PIRATE'S PROMISE

The Legend of Caesar Creek

B. William Hoolihan

Publisher Name: Sabal Palm Press

Print ISBN: 978-1-969718-01-4
LCCN: 2025912023

Credits:
     Cover Design Copyright © Michael Dorer

This book is dedicated to George.

PREFACE

The goal of Spanish explorers was to steal treasure for their insolvent homeland. They excelled in this mission and stole mind-boggling quantities from Native Americans. From the sixteenth to the eighteenth century, this treasure would be transported twice a year across the Atlantic Ocean to Spain. Simultaneously, international commerce increased along the shores of the Americas. Vessels filled with all forms of commodities and valuables traveled north and south, in sight of land, and perilously close to reefs, rocks and sandbars. To some, they were prey... and where there is prey, there will always be predators.

PROLOGUE

Summer 1718
Elliott Key, Florida

After serving a hellish year in His Majesty's Carolina prison, young Smith made his way to the port of Charleston. He walked the docks night and day trying to beg, borrow or steal his way on board a southbound vessel. Touting his blacksmithing skills, he eventually landed a berth on board the *Triton*, a schooner headed to Cayo Hueso, the westernmost of the Florida Keys. Prior to arriving at the vessel's port of call he planned to steal a dinghy (he was a pirate after all) and return to Elliott Key as Caesar, his pirate mentor, instructed.

Caesar was the most important figure in the boy's life. He was a father figure and much more. He was a teacher, a guide; he taught Smith how to survive on the ocean and land and even saved his life on more than one occasion. Caesar was a pirate but no heathen. It was rumored he was African royalty, and many a night he, Smith and a Tequesta named Kalos would sit around the campfire and ponder the stars and the universe and the enormity of life. And so, it became Smith's life's mission to fulfill Caesar's last wish. A life he would gladly trade to ensure that Caesar legacy was fulfilled.

~~~

In the Bay of Campeche off the coast of Mexico, conditions were ripe for the birth of one of nature's most impressive creations. The water was warm; the winds were light and giant, black anvil clouds began to form. And rain. Torrents of blinding rain. The fallen rain would be heated by the warm ocean and returned to the clouds in an ominous, seemingly never-ending cycle. One of many cycles that repeat endlessly in nature.

The entire system began to slowly spiral and march eastward, its sights set on South Florida. A hurricane of immense power and ferocity was born and ready to sink, flood or destroy anything in its path.

~~~

The schooner was making good time and Smith's duties were limited, so he spent hours watching frigate birds turn and wheel in the sky performing their ballet of aerial piracy and observing a myriad of sea birds feeding on shoals of baitfish. The easterly breeze held and soon they passed St. Augustine. In two more days, they would be abreast of Cayo Vizcayne and then Elliott Key. Soon Smith could put his plan in motion.

When not watching the ocean and its sea life,

Smith stayed close to the captain on the stern deck. His name was Haynes, and he hailed from Boston. Smith had hoped to learn some rudimentary navigation from him, but that was not to be. The captain was a good man, but his seafaring experience was limited to coastal sailing, usually in sight of land. His navigation method consisted of watching the coastline for landmarks, taking bearings and checking the depth and bottom composition.

The monthly run to Cayo Hueso was relatively simple, especially compared to ocean crossings. On the south run, Captain Haynes would lie close to the lee shore to escape the northbound Gulfstream current. On his return northward, he would venture further out to seek the swift-moving indigo waters, which could save up to two days off his trip. He told Smith the trip was safe except when you passed Saint Augustine; you had to watch out for sudden storms and pirates. Either could seemingly pop out of nowhere. Smith smiled and inwardly thought, *If you only knew. matey. If you only knew.*

As the *Triton* continued its southern journey, the masthead lookout saw the squall line and alerted the captain. He viewed it through his spyglass and, although it appeared ominous, he wasn't particularly alarmed. The *Triton* was on a schedule, and he saw no reason to reduce sail. The line of storms was on them quickly and all aboard realized this was no ordinary squall.

Captain Haynes ultimately shouted the order to reduce sail, but it was too late. The shrieking winds shredded the sails like old rags. One sail after the other. A sickening, tearing sound. To those knowledgeable on board, this was the sound of a dying ship. Within minutes, the vessel looked ghostly, with its once billowing sails reduced to streaming tatters. The funeral flags of a ship about to sink. Without the sails, they would lose steerage and be at the storm's mercy.

The captain bellowed order after order, but either he could not be heard over the winds, or his sailors simply chose to ignore his commands. The ship was in a state of chaos, facing seventy-five-mile-an-hour winds and waves growing to twenty feet. Some sailors were praying, and others broke into the spirit locker, believing it best to drown in a drunken stupor. None could swim.

Smith now realized the flaw in Haynes's navigational strategy. By running so close to the coast in shallow waters, he had nowhere to run. The shallow water that had previously offered him refuge now caused the waves to rise up much higher than if they were sailing further offshore. The *Triton* had no escape route. They were trapped even if the sails held.

The sun was obscured and the schooner began to broach. This violent action caused the stays to snap and the masts came down with a mighty crash just as they did when they were felled in the northern forests of Europe. The deck soon became impassable with broken masts, yard arms, cordage, nets, the injured and the dead.

Smith grabbed Captain Haynes by the arm and yelled, "Captain! The ship is lost. The dinghy in the stern davits hasn't been stove in yet. We must leave. Join me, I implore you."

Haynes turned to Smith slowly. He was in shock and Smith knew he'd be of no help. Captain Haynes was as dead as his eyes; he just didn't know it yet.

Smith ran awkwardly to the stern, trying to balance on the wildly pitching deck. It was a miracle she hadn't broached yet. He needed one more minute. Just one. The dinghy was swinging dangerously and there was no hope of launching it from the twisted and useless davits. He grabbed a length of line and tied one end around his waist. With the other he was able to lasso the dinghy's stanchion. It would have to do. He cut the bow and stern davit lines and she fell into the violent sea like an anchor…with Smith attached.

The boy plunged violently beneath the

turbulent water and then fought his way to the surface for air. When he emerged, he witnessed an unimaginable sight. The schooner was now broadside to a monster wave, sliding sideways down its monstrous face to its underwater grave. Smith desperately tried to escape the mayhem by pushing and kicking the wreckage around him. He tried and tried, but the dinghy and he were entangled in a mass of broken rigging. As the boy's head went under, he caught sight of a ghostly Caesar and desperately reached for the oar the apparition extended. Just as Caesar had done one dark night, a lifetime ago.

~~~

The hurricane tore into the outer reef with one hundred and fifty mile per hour winds and thirty-foot waves. Sea creatures and birds deserted days before, using their innate instinct to avoid bad weather. Even the majority of bottom-hugging lobsters headed for deeper waters, and those that remained hunkered down in deep holes and inside shelters like brain corals. The horrifying storm then moved onshore, creating more devastation. It rerouted Elliott Key's east channel, uprooted mangroves and wiped away any trace of the pirates' camp. It was inconceivable that a band of buccaneers had at one time existed there. The wharf, tents, campfire pits and treasure building had simply vanished from the face of the earth.
~~~

Nothing remained. Except Smith's metallic handiwork twisted tightly into the ground and, further up the key, a large block of limestone with nascent carvings resembling a sea turtle.

Within weeks, hardy, time-tested vegetation sprouted infantile leaves and nature began a cycle that had been repeating for time without end. Over the next three hundred years the mangroves, sea grapes and saw palmetto grew, died, and grew again until the only remaining evidence of the pirates' existence was hidden by impenetrable vegetation.

PART ONE
ONE

Summer 1967
Coconut Grove, Florida

Damn George! My rusty hammer just hit the corroded chisel and backfired painfully into my hand! Sweat was pouring off my head, stinging my eyes, and my faded little league cap couldn't hold back the sweltering, steamy Florida day. Nothing could stop this muggy heat. Tired, dirty and frustrated, I took a breath and shouted, "What the hell is your house made of?"

"A pier," was the indifferent reply.

Huh? I thought.

My instructions were to cut a twelve-inch hole in the side of George's house. Any way I could. I had broken through plaster and now hit some nasty, primeval wood. Really hard, pitch-black timber that oozed resin and smelled like creosote.

"C'mon, George. A pier? What darn pier?"

"Haulover Pier. The '47 hurricane knocked it down."

"What's it doing in your house?"

"After the storm I hauled the pilings here, built the house out of 'em. By myself. Price was right. Seemed like a great idea," he chuckled.

Okay, let that set in a bit. The man, George Henderson, after surviving a deadly hurricane, drove to Haulover Beach, went into the surf, lashed chains around monstrous fallen pilings, dragged them fifteen miles back to Coconut Grove and built a bomb shelter of a log cabin he then slathered in plaster. The whole thing reminded me of that guy in Homestead who erected Coral Castle out of blocks of limestone…by himself.

Why was I trying to lose a finger that day?

It was the first day of summer and my mother told me to find a job. Slinging burgers, bagging groceries or selling mangoes didn't interest me one bit. In fact, the Haden brothers, down the street, seemed to have the mango market covered. She mentioned that George, a "colorful neighbor," needed help on a variety of projects and I thought, why not? Put a little muscle on my skinny arms and get a tan to boot. But I needed to be paid in cash, not beer and cigarettes like the last time.

Over Christmas break I built a ribbon driveway for him using plywood, lengths of one-by-twos, a saw and, wait for it … a hatchet. I ordered the concrete trucks by lowering my voice and pretending I was a man. The funny thing was, I ended up Huck Finning the whole project. My friends would ride by on their bikes, and if they got off to inspect, I had them! Cheap labor. Thank goodness the shrimpers at Dinner Key Marina bought George's contraband payment from me.

Anyhow, I stopped by his house, and he said

he had a bunch of summer projects he could use a hand with. He was vague, though, when I asked him to define projects. So, my first chore with George was to break a hole in the side of his casa de creosote, so we could hook up a new septic tank.

"How, George? With what tools?"

"Jeesh," he said, "if I knew, then I'd do it myself."

Hard to argue with that kind of logic. So, I scoured his tool shed, which meant his yard with rusty junk scattered everywhere. I found some chisels and hammers and went to work. By the end of the job, I sharpened a car leaf spring, which I hit with a sledgehammer to break through the pilings.

When I was done, George observed the hole. "I knew you could do it, Billy. Don't doubt yourself. Brains beat brawn." As we sat there, he said, "Beer?" and offered me a cold can of brew.

"No, thanks, George."

He looked puzzled and then said, "Camel?" and offered me a cigarette.

"No, thanks."

"Well, you're a real drip." Then he smiled and said, "How're your grades?"

"Straight As, George."

To which he simply replied, "Okay."

As I was hopping on my avocado-colored Schwinn to ride home, George shouted, "Watcha doing tomorrow?"

"Nothing important. Why?"

"Great. We're going on a field trip. I'll see ya

at eight. Bring your mask and fins. Some Vienna sausages too."

TWO

Riding my bike always gave me time to contemplate. I thought this could be the greatest summer of my life. Or the worst. I had grand designs for my future, but I was also riddled with teenage angst and insecurity. George was one of the wildest, most interesting people I had ever met in my sum of fifteen years. He was smart and always had a wild tale to tell or was about to embark on some crazy Caribbean adventure.

I had no male figure in my life, and while George might not have been the epitome of fatherhood, I was drawn to him. He drank a bit, smoked too much and cussed like a sailor. No, that's wrong, he cussed way better than a sailor. He invented cuss words. His cuss words had cuss words. But he had a good heart. And he presented an alternate view of the world that didn't look like the Cleaver's or even the Brady's.

George was a good-looking guy, in a rugged kind of way. Mid-fifties but looked forties. Dirty-blond hair, chiseled features and crow's-feet with mischievous, twinkly, often bloodshot eyes. Permanent mahogany tan. Kind of a cross between Steve McQueen and Clint Eastwood. His voice was New England, with a hint of Caymanian. It was a pleasant voice, engaging and authoritative.

Not a great dresser, though. Think of a modern-day Robinson Crusoe look, which might explain why he was a lifelong bachelor. I'm sure there were women who thought they could change him, but it would be easier to break a hole through a house built from a pier. Damn near impossible.

Where did his wanderlust for Caribbean adventure stem from? He never came right out and told me, but he spent World War II in Key West working in a Seabee construction battalion. After a hard day working in the sun, I could picture him wandering to the local bars treading carefully in Hemingway's drunken footsteps, soaking in the rum and the local tales of shipwrecks, pirates and legends.

Me? I was a skinny teenager living with my mom, who was a second-grade teacher in a nearby elementary school. Her pay was rotten, but she took the job so we could spend summers together. I was gregarious, but also a bit self-conscious at six foot three and 160 pounds with rocks in my pockets. My bell bottoms were a little short and my shirtsleeves, too. It didn't bother me much that we didn't have much money, but my outdated and ill-fitting clothing set me apart from the cool kids. Kids that were my best friends in elementary school, where no one really cared what you wore, now became distant. So, I was a bit of an outcast in junior high, but also confident enough to know that, as good friends do, they would return one day.

Money was always an issue, so I tried to help

out by taking odd jobs. I was handier than most kids. To save money for college, I planned to go to the Naval Academy. Seemed like a sweet gig to me. Sail their beautiful boats all day. They'd be lucky to have a guy like me.

The more I thought about it, the deeper my feeling became that this would be the greatest summer of my life.

THREE

As I walked out the door the next morning, my mom asked what George and I were up to. *Uh, working on his boat,* which was technically true. I didn't want her to worry her, as she had enough on her plate. I made it to George's, where he promptly offered me a cigarette.

"No, thanks, George."

"Beer?"

"Nah, I'm good."

"Ah, a bourbon man. I like your style, Billy Boy."

"George, I don't drink."

To that, he muttered something that sounded like "Commie pussy."

After having my emerging manhood impugned, I hitched up his beat-up boat and trailer to his car, known as the Purple Haze. I had named it this because the fading of the maroon color turned into a psychedelic purple, and it needed a valve job, so it was frequently clouded in a haze of exhaust.

"Where to, Captain?" I asked.

"Well, I'm craving lobster, so let's head down south to the reefs off Soldier Key. I hear they're everywhere."

"George, I don't know how to catch lobster."

"How hard could it be?" was the reply.

We launched out of Matheson Hammock, crossed Biscayne Bay to Boca Chita and wound our way through an unmarked finger channel, where we began looking for reefs. We viewed them through a five-gallon bucket with a piece of clear plexiglass in the bottom that George designed. He also showed me a method where you turned the boat sharply at low speed and at the stern there would be a small patch of clear water with no ripples, like a sheet of glass, and you could see all the way to the bottom. We finally found a good-looking reef in thirty feet of water where we even saw lobsters walking on two brain corals.

George downed a beer while I slowly put my fins and flippers on and said, "Now what?" He handed me a net and a short metal stick and a miniature red scuba tank. "George, I don't scuba dive."

"You should. It's a lot of fun."

"Okay, I'll try, but did you ... make that?"

"Yep. It's an old fire extinguisher. Beauty, ain't she?"

Before I could object, he strapped the faded red tank on my back, put the regulator in my mouth, handed me a net and stick, and pushed me overboard. I sputtered at the surface and asked what I was supposed to do.

"Breathe," he said, "and don't hold your breath. And push lobsters into the net." And with that sage advice, I descended to the reef below.

Gosh, it was beautiful. Above the reef there were multiple schools of fish with each unique group moving as one. Blue runners, yellowtail, French grunts. The reef was full of sponges, fans and corals, and dominated by two brain corals on the south end, perhaps twenty-five feet across. Jacks, hogfish and angelfish were swimming in all directions. And clawless lobsters everywhere. Technically they're a large crawfish, hence the lack of claws. But Miamians are good at putting a positive spin on things. I mean, just look at the history of Miami Beach. It took me a bit, but eventually I created a technique to tickle them into the net. It was hard to keep them in, though. They would circle around at high speed, then fly out. In the back of my mind I was devising a second bag where they went in but couldn't get out.

Eventually I was able to encourage some of the slower crustaceans to remain and I was both excited and frustrated, so I headed up to the silhouetted boat. I handed George the net with lobsters and stick. As I started to climb up the stern, I felt a twinge in my elbow.

"George, is my arm supposed to hurt?"

"No. Did you come up too quick?"

"I might have."

He pushed me back in the water. I sputtered once again and asked what I should do.

"Go sit on the bottom for a bit and next time don't come up faster than your bubbles."

"What if I run out of air? There's no gauge."

George said, "Well, I'd come up then, but that's just me."

I smiled nervously, kicked back down to the bottom and sat on a flat-topped rock by the brain coral, which was covered in algae. It was fun watching the lively reef like my own personal aquarium. I watched a large moray eel survey the bottom of the brain coral for nooks and crevices before settling into his new abode.

Then I felt a strange feeling. Hard to describe. Something watching me. I shivered, saw a shadow on the sand and then I saw it. It was George; he dove down in his boxers and shoes. He stared at me and popped open a beer, took a swig, put his thumb over the opening and offered it to me. I laughed so hard I spit out my regulator. Which didn't matter as the tank had just run out of air. We surfaced together and laughed till we practically cried.

As we sat in the boat and watched the lobsters scatter about the deck, George asked what I was doing tonight. I told him I didn't have any plans, so he said he would see me at seven.

"I want to run something by you over grilled lobsters, corn, baked potatoes and Key lime pie."

"I'll be there." My mom, God love her, made "Something Helper" every night of the week, and a real man dinner sounded like heaven to my ever-rumbling belly.

"Hey, did you notice the rock I was sitting on? It was different. Not really coral," I said.

"Yep, I did. They reminded me of the rocks we

discovered off Bimini in '53. People say they may be the Steps to Atlantis."

George continued his Bimini story chaotically over many beers as I steered us home, munching on Vienna sausages. I felt great on the ocean, kind of like a pirate. No rules, live off the sea. Use your wits. Out here it was so much better than on land.

It was the first week of summer 1967. The Summer of Love. Woodstock, Timothy Leary, *Hair*, drugs and hippies. And Coconut Grove was Haight-Ashbury south. Hippies everywhere. Most were sincere. Artsy rebels trying to make the world a better place. They would spend all day in Peacock Park, play guitar and smoke marijuana when the police weren't around.

But all was not groovy, so to speak. Bad news was delivered from trusting men with silk voices inside glass tubes or on your morning breakfast table in black and white. There was the Vietnam War, the threat of Cold War, Russians in Cuba, missiles based in South Florida. The world was scary, but we were seemingly sheltered in the Grove.

Coconut Grove was an iconic section of Miami. Lush and tropical and kissed by Biscayne Bay on its long southeastern border. Many of the first Miamians had settled here not only because of the bay access but also because the land was slightly higher than the sea-level landscape of most of South Florida. This ten-to-fifteen-foot elevation could make the difference between life and death when a hurricane threatened.

Miami was a magical city. But the summers were an acquired taste that required a subtle acclimatization. We drank from hoses and endured daily thunderstorms that were followed by cool, ozone-tinted air. The smell of freshly cut grass, iced tea with Key lime ice cubes, eating sweet, juicy mangoes. These were the things that came with summer in the Grove.

FOUR

After a quick shower and watching a casserole go from box to oven, I kissed my mom goodbye, hopped on my bike and rode over to George's. His cooking technique consisted of building a big fire, tossing aluminum-clad food in the coals and then sitting back and having a couple of beers. Yes, aluminum. George took pride in using the British terms for many objects. As in a crankshaft was a bumpy stick. No timer, no recipe; just some of the best-tasting food I ever had in my life. When I couldn't eat another bite, he brought out a perfectly chilled Key lime pie.

After the meal, George and I were just watching the coals die down and he got serious. "I want to tell you something, Billy. I know most folks think I'm a dreamer and immature and all that. Chasing windmills and such. But life's too short to wear a suit and tie and work in a dehumidified and dehumanized office. Life should be an adventure. It's a big world, man. So much to see and do. I think you get that. I think you'll understand what I'm about to tell you."

"What's that, George?"

"Have you ever heard of Black Caesar?"

"Nope."

"Ever heard of Caesar Creek?"

"Sure, just south of Elliott Key, but I've never been through it."

"Well, it's named after a pirate who was called Black Caesar and thought to be an escaped slave from Africa. As the legend goes, he camped on the north side of the creek, and when opportunity presented itself, he would sail out and capture small vessels and salvage others that had run aground. He made a good living from this and it's believed Blackbeard himself paid him a visit. I guess he wanted to check out the competition, and it's a fact Blackbeard was based in Nassau at the same time.

"Blackbeard apparently persuaded Caesar to sail up to North Carolina to help plunder the local shipping, which was more prevalent than off Elliott Key."

"And did he?"

"Yes, sir. But it had a tragic ending with a battle where Blackbeard was killed, and Caesar was supposedly captured and hanged."

"Do you think he left any treasure behind?" I asked.

"Well, it would make sense to me. If I were going to leave a relatively safe haven and join Blackbeard, I would have left some behind. Like a retirement plan, so to speak."

"George, they would need a small sloop to get in and out of there, which requires a mast and sails. And a mast would stick up way beyond the mangroves and alert anyone with a spyglass to see them."

"Listen to you. That's right! The legend says they buried an iron ring on shore and used it with block and tackle to pull the mast down out of sight."

"George, please, please tell me you have a treasure map!"

"No, I don't, but I believe the ring exists."

"Really, George? C'mon, man, spill the beans," I demanded.

George went on. "Well, about ten years ago I was having a hangover breakfast at a diner on Long Key called the Red Caboose. Best hash browns around and a certified hangover cure. I started chatting with a couple who lived on nearby Lignum Vitae Key. After a bit, Charlotte and Russell Niedhauk told me that they had lived on Sands Key, in the mid-1930s, just north of Elliott Key. We got to talking about shipwrecks, wreckers and eventually pirates. After a bit, Russell slowly looked around the diner to see if we were out of earshot of the other customers. Feeling assured, he slowly began to reveal what he knew about the legend of Black Caesar and the existence of the iron ring. He had heard the legend from a mysterious Miccosukee, who visited them one day in his cypress log canoe.

"I said to Russell, 'Do you think the story is true?' 'Darn tootin' I do.' 'Why's that?' I asked. ''Cause I found the ring. Well, at least I think I did,' was his reply.

"Russell went on to explain. He and Charlotte, after hearing about the legend, spent some time exploring all the nearby islands for pirate treasure. Not an easy task as they were dense with all manner of vegetation. In the summer of 1935, fleeing birds and animals told them a big storm was coming—perhaps a hurricane. Russell needed lumber to shore up their house, so he went down to Caesar Creek, where driftwood and actual lumber often got caught in the mangroves. It was a good day at the 'store,' as he liked to call it, and as he was loading his skiff, he spied the ring through the mangroves. It was hard to see, but he was sure that was it. He wanted to come back after the storm, but it was so devastating that they left the island and never returned."

"Why did he tell you?"

"Well, he felt the treasure wasn't there. No caves and the ground was too hard and rocky to dig a significant hole. But he did believe there must be a clue somewhere. His treasure-hunting days were over, but he said with a gleam in his eye that perhaps mine had just begun. With that, the couple paid their tab, smiled, said, '*Vaya con Dios, mi amigo*,' and walked out.

"So, Billy, now I'm telling you. I want to find the ring this summer. If we do, then I'm confident there must be treasure clues to find also. I have a feeling there's something there. It's hard to explain, but I feel it in my soul. I'm not young anymore. Too much rum, whiskey and these damn cancer sticks. I'm getting tired. And you're young and sharp. You may see something I don't."

"Wow, George! A pirate adventure! Sure, I'll help. I was thinking. We've been covering colonial American history in school. If there was a hanging, there was a trial. And if there was trial, there may be a record of it."

George said, "You're probably right. But why is that important?"

"Well …" I thought out loud. "If we can prove Caesar existed on paper, then that will give us the momentum to start changing the legend into a fact. So we don't feel like we're chasing a ghost."

"Or a duppy," George muttered. "So how do you plan to get court records from three hundred years ago?"

"Well, that's where my mom comes in. She's an officer in a historical society. Those ladies love researching stuff like this. Let me see if she can help."

"Great idea, Billy. See, I knew I made the right choice," he said, smiling.

As I left, I thought that, with George's tale, the Summer of Love had just gotten a whole lot better.

FIVE

Later that night I walked through my avocado-colored front door, in my avocado-colored house and stepped onto the avocado-colored carpet. I was met by the ubiquitous sound of Herb Albert and his Tijuana Brass. My mom loved Herb Albert. He and the Brass were upbeat, Latin-tinged, and distracted her from the toils of being a single mother in the 1960s. The era was known for psychedelic music, but I grew fond of Herb's music and to this day when I hear "A Taste of Honey" I'm instantly transported to summertime in Miami. And don't get a teenage boy started on the album cover! I also wondered if the Baja Marimba Band was to the Tijuana Brass like the Stones were to the Beatles. Kind of their bad boy alter ego.

Mom was in the kitchen, about to make a Key lime pie. "Just one?" I questioned. My mom's Key lime pies were excellent and rivaled George's. I'd been known to eat half of one before baseball practice and the other half afterward.

"Yes, just one!" she replied. "I swear, I don't know where you put it. So, Bill William, how are things with George? Getting a lot done?"

"Yes, ma'am. Lots. Very productive."

"Well, don't let him pay you in beer. Or cigarettes!! I've heard stories, young man."

"I won't. Listen, Mom, I need your help. George is working on genealogy project and perhaps your Sisters of the American Revolution can help?"

"Well, it's called the Daughters of the American Revolution, DAR for short. And I guess it's possible. What does he need?"

So, I spent the next thirty minutes squeezing Key limes and explaining about Black Caesar trial.

When I finished, she said, "So, George thinks there were pirates in Miami. My goodness. Next, he'll be telling you his Cayman Island duppy stories. I'll write some letters and see what I can find out. Pirates, I swear."

~~~

The summer wasn't going to be all fun and games around George's house—or as he referred to it, Shangri-La. The compound consisted of several small buildings, all in need of varying degrees of restoration. The first was his house, the second an attached office, and he had a third that was an apartment he rented to, shall we say, an assortment of colorful figures. The structures were surrounded by two acres of lush landscaping that would be described as pre-Tequesta Everglades. He believed in the natural look. He even constructed a turtle pond right in the middle of his lot. He said their presence calmed him down.

One of my many jobs was head landscaper.
~~~

The goal was to keep the zoning and code enforcement guys at bay by keeping the grass, a.k.a. weeds, to a manageable level using George's 1950 B&S blue-smoke-belching lawn mower.

Simply pushing it had little effect on the stubborn undergrowth. I had to invent my own technique of pushing down on the handle, which raised the front of the mower, attacking the enemy from above. The only problem with this method of constantly raising the mower up and down, as George later explained, was air would get in the gas line and the engine would conk out. But he showed me how to prime the line and the process would repeat. About the only good thing about mowing was the smell of fresh-cut grass. It's the chlorophyll in the air, but it smelled like nature's perfume to me.

George had a variety of fruit trees and let me tell you, when you're hot and sweaty, a mango tastes like nirvana right off the tree. You don't even notice that the juice is running everywhere. George let me eat all the mangoes I wanted. Sometimes he'd lean out a window and yell in a crazy Jamaican accent, "Eat, mon, eat. Dey be good for da bamboo, mon." I never knew what he was talking about until I visited Jamaica as an adult.

After a hard day of mowing, I liked to sit in the shade and listen to the wind whistle through the Australian pines. At the same time, I enjoyed the gurgle of the water bubbling in his pond as his crazy turtles wandered about. It was peaceful, almost primordial. The Grove was Miami's enchanted forest and George managed to create a sanctuary within its confines. Perhaps even a modern-day pirate lair.

SIX

I always liked to start my day off with a cup of Joe and the Miami *Tribune*, the local newspaper. Still do. Bob of the "Bob Is Here" fruit stand once told me, "In order to have a productive day, you have to see the sunrise." Well, teenagers and sunrises are like oil and water, but I did feel the same way about my coffee and newspaper. On this particular day, I was engrossed in an article involving Elliott Key.

I said *whoa* to myself, ripped out the article, kissed Mom goodbye and rushed over to George's. I found him looking for the answers to life in his own coffee cup.

"Cigarette?"

"No, thanks, George. Listen, have you read the paper?"

"Nah, I can't trust those guys. They just do it for the money. Beer?"

"No, thanks, George. Listen, George, focus. This is important. Elliott Key, or rather Islandia, is in the paper."

"Huh? What's it say?"

"Well, first of all, did you know a developer was trying to put hotels and golf courses there?"

"Yeah, Richard Little. He's an asshole's asshole. But the feds wouldn't approve permits for him to build bridges from Key Biscayne to Elliott, so he was screwed. Couldn't happen to a nicer guy."

"You know 'em?"

"Yep. But what else?"

"The article says exactly that, and the Park Service is seizing the island for park land."

"Good. Screw him!"

"Yes, but now he's bulldozing the whole island before the turnover date. Already cut a road right down the middle that the Trib is calling Spite Road."

"Damn, you think he's looking for treasure? Or clues? We've got to get there and do our own investigation."

"Okay. Let's head over tomorrow and see what we can dig up."

With that, I fired up the lawn mower and started my daily routine of mow, sweat, stall, prime, repeat. My summertime quartet.

~~~

Later that day I dehydratedly staggered in my front door and was promptly escorted back out by a highly agitated schoolteacher. Apparently, Mom's avocado-green decor did not extend to her hardworking son, who was covered in wet green grass. It was even staining my skin, much like that indigo-colored tribe in Africa called the Taureg. Mom told me to rinse off outside with the garden
~~~

hose, leave my clothes and sneakers by the side door and only then was I allowed in with just a towel she threw at me.

After my shower, I snuck a piece of Key lime pie and was going to grab a catnap when she said, "Billy, a letter arrived from the Virginia DAR today."

"What's its say, Ma?"

"My, those nice ladies took all that time. My goodness. Wasn't that nice, Billy?"

"Mom, what did it say? It's important!"

"Okay. Don't be in such a huff, young man. She says yes, there was a pirate trial in Williamsburg in 1718, and there's a list of prisoners and their sentences. What colorful names. Paddy Nine Fingers. Spanish Johnny."

"Ma, I don't care about them! Was there a Caesar?"

"I swear, you are so impatient, young man."

"I'm sorry, Ma. It's just very important!"

"Let's see. Yes, here it is. It says Captain Caesar, escaped slave. Death by hanging. How horrible! All were convicted and hanged. Except a boy. This is all kind of gruesome. Maybe you shouldn't be spending so much time with Mr. Henderson."

"No, Mom, it's fine. George is a great boss and he's teaching me a lot. He's paying me in cash too." *And not contraband*, I thought. "In fact, here's twenty bucks, Mom."

"Why, thank you, Billy. I do appreciate you

helping out. We'll be okay once school starts, and I'll pay you back every cent."

"That's okay, Mom."

That night it was hard to sleep pondering all the pirate possibilities.

SEVEN

Neither George nor I were particularly early-morning people, but we managed an early start after his obligatory offering and my polite refusal of beer and cigarettes, and we were soon gliding across the bay in his skiff. I filled George in on the DAR news and then we both lapsed into our own thoughts as we headed to the Featherbed Banks. From there we would pass through a narrow channel and head south to Elliott Key.

After thirty minutes, we ran the boat up on a flat on the southwest side of the island. As we waded ashore, I was reminded of the scene in *Dr. No* where James Bond and Honey Ryder visit secretive Crab Key. George was a terrible Ursula Andress. Ursula Andress! Wet, sun-streaked hair, teeny white bikini, white web belt with dive knife. Holding a conch. My bubbling teenage hormones were displaced by a robust odor. The sulfur smell of a mangrove swamp at low tide mixed with a clean, salt-filled breeze. Not unpleasant, but enough to cruelly shake Ursula out of mind.

George and I wandered around for a bit. The mosquitoes were awful, and it was quite desolate except for the freshly carved scar right down the middle of the island. We were walking south on the Spite Road toward the area where Mr. Niedhauk had found the ring when we heard shouting from behind us. We both turned around and observed a short bald man running towards us. The term *running* was a stretch. More like a wobble-trot. He was comically wearing a homemade police officer's uniform (think Buford T. Justice) and yelling something about trespassing on his Islandia. We would have laughed except he was waving a pistol that eventually went off. Bam! George and I took off for the boat and I was hoping he had only one bullet, like Barney Fife. Bam. Nope, I guess he didn't work for Sheriff Andy.

George and I practically dove in the boat and got the heck outta there. "Who the hell was that?" I gasped.

An equally out-of-breath George replied, "That, young Bill, was Dick Little. Mayor and apparently Chief of Police of Islandia. And truly a dick's dick."

~~~

When we got back to Shangri-La we held a debriefing over beer, coffee and Key lime pie. You can guess who had what. I started off by asking George how he knew our Elliott Key nemesis.

"Well, like I said, that was Richard Little, but everybody calls him Dick. If the shoe fits, ya know. And he sure seems up to something.

"He made his start in the real estate business by foreclosing on residents of the west Grove area.
~~~

Did you know that area was originally settled by Bahamians?"

"Nope," I replied, "but how did he do it?"

"Well, if a homeowner can't afford to pay their property taxes, then the county allows 'businessmen' to loan them the money at eighteen percent. And if they don't pay up, then the house is foreclosed and a bloodsucker like Little gets it.

"He started that monkey business with a sweet old lady everyone called Miss Jane. She owned a house near the business district and for that reason one day it would be worth a lot of money. And Little knew that. Anyhow, when I found out Little was foreclosing on Miss Jane, I loaned her the tax money. At first, she wouldn't accept it, but we eventually came to an arrangement. Miss Jane has dropped off a loaf of Bimini bread every Sunday since. I've told her to stop, but, darn, it tastes like it was just made in Alice Town.

"The aptly named Dick is a sneaky you know what and knows how to make a buck. And he hates my guts. He was already counting his chickens with Miss Jane's property. I hit him where it hurt him the most, in his moth-eaten wallet.

"We've got to find a way to get back on Elliott Key, but he's on to us too. He'll alert whatever people he has working there. We need to be clever. Regardless, it's going to be difficult."

George and I were both frustrated. We knew something was there. We could feel it in our bones. And for Little to end up with it was just plain wrong. We were at a stalemate, so we temporarily reverted to our summer routine of me sweating in George's yard and George working on a cockamamie plan.

EIGHT

One particularly hot day, George took pity on me and suggested I get some smoothies from a new health food store called The Last Carrot. As I rode over I wondered if George would add a dark rum floater to his.

When I walked in, I was greeted by the trippy sound of "Magical Mystery Tour" emanating from a sweet-sounding eight-track stereo, followed by the sugary aroma of fresh-cut fruit with a hint of patchouli oil. There were a lot of dudes in front of me, so I poked around a bit. When it was my turn to order, I was spellbound by the girl behind the counter. No wonder all the guys were here. She was tall, Nordic-looking, long blond hair with a flower in it.

Before I could order, she said in a sweet voice, "Well, aren't you working hard?"

I wondered how she knew that until I noticed my reflection in a glass case. Sweat-stained, sun-burned and—oh, St. Augustine grass here and there. As if I wasn't self-conscious enough.

"Uh, yeah," I stammered. "I own a landscape service."

"Really! What's it called?"

"Natural Beauty," I said and gave her a wink. She smiled a big smile and went on to take my order.

When I left, she yelled out, "Hey, landscaper, don't be a stranger!"

When I got back to George's and finally sipped the smoothie, I couldn't believe how good it was. Even George was impressed.

"How'd did you hear about it?" I asked.

George said, "My neighbor Dave. Ya know, the guy who owns Gwendolyn the alligator."

"What!" I replied.

George said, "Yeah, he's got a ten-foot pet alligator named Gwendolyn. Raised it from a baby. Damn thing would sit in your lap if you let it. Anyhow, he goes all the time to the Last Carrot."

"Well, George, you wouldn't believe the girl who works there. I was shaking just standing there talking to her. I've never seen her around."

"Hmm," George said. "If I were you, I'd make more smoothie runs, then."

With that I fired up Ol' Smokey, my new name for the lawn mower, and daydreamed lascivious thoughts about Smoothie Girl.

~~~

George's love advice was sound, and I found myself frequenting The Last Carrot. Smoothie Girl's name was Noelle and her family had recently moved to the Grove. Her dad was in the foreign service, and they'd just returned from a posting in France. She didn't really have many friends, but
~~~

that was changing fast. I wasn't the only guy who suddenly developed a liking for tuna melts with sprouts and tahini sauce.

The last time I was at the Carrot there was a red convertible Camaro in the parking lot. Uh-oh. Joe Goodwin. Football jock. Big man on campus. Dumb as a hammer. He'd spell Caesar as Seize Her. She was talking to him. More like flirt-talking. Sweeping her hair back, giggling, over emoting. How can I compete with him? I couldn't bear to stick around, so I left.

I slinked into George's yard empty-handed and he asked what happened. I told him how popular she was becoming, and I was giving up my pursuit. Then George verbally kicked my ass. He said she'd be lucky to go out with me. Told me I had the whole world in front of me. I was smart, tall, and funny. Hell, sometimes even confident.

After his pep talk, I returned to the Carrot. I even started walking Noelle home on occasion. She didn't have a car either. We shared a lot. She told me about Paris, Joni Mitchell and macrobiotic cooking. And I told her about George and our adventures. At first, I was vague, but she was totally enthralled and pressed me for details until she knew almost as much as I did. It was nice to confide in someone about our quest. I knew the whole Caesar legend was a half-crazy idea, but it was nice to know someone other than George thought it was a worthwhile mission too.

NINE

George and I were in pirate limbo. We couldn't make a move. Stalemate. He had some clues from the Neidhauks and the DAR information from the Williamsburg trial, but we were at loggerheads with the situation. One morning he called before I headed over. He gave me some cursory details of a plan to get back to Elliott Key and said that we'd be gone for a day or two.

As I walked out the door, I told Mom that we were going on a rescue mission to help a stranded sailor in the Keys. Might have to stay out overnight. I explained that George was on a mission of mercy.

"That's very nice of him. Now I feel bad about mistrusting him," she said. "Just be careful. I'll have a pie ready when you get home."

On the way down to Key Largo, George explained the "plan" in more detail. He had a friend, Bronx Al, from, you guessed it … Philly, who was sailing to South America. Something about an affair with a mob wife. But now he was stranded at the Ocean Reef Motel on Key Largo. It was a small motel, but a wide-eyed developer had big plans for it. Al and his "Pride of the Hudson" had limped into the fledging resort with torn sails and a missing propeller due to a small run-in with a misplaced reef. Eventually he wore out his welcome by being an eyesore to potential clients and extremely delinquent on his dock fees. So, George was going to help him put on a new prop, then limp back to Miami for cheap repairs and a free mooring off Dinner Key. Oh, and a stopover at Elliott Key.

We hit the Winn-Dixie for provisions, which consisted of four cases of beer, a loaf of white bread, peanut butter and jelly. All the essential food groups. We drove down Card Sound Road past a biker bar called 'Bama Jacks and over the newly constructed Card Sound Bridge. Man, what a far-out view. You could see forever up there, even Elliott Key, our destination.

We pulled up to the "Pride" and it was in worse shape than I'd thought. Sixty-seven feet of nautical chaos.

"Uh, George what the heck is this boat made of?"

"Concrete! Can you believe it?"

"Who the heck makes a boat out of concrete? And, oh, I'm not going anywhere on this fuckin' death trap!"

"Billy, I'll have you know that ferro cement is a time-honored boat-building material."

"Really?! Who thought of this? The lead balloon guys?"

"Very funny. During World War II, the US military couldn't spare steel for supply ships, so this method was invented. You've heard of the concrete boat off South Bimini. The SS *Sapona*. Well, it's famous and it's a concrete boat."

"Yeah, how's it doing?" I asked.

"Uh, it sunk," he said with a crooked smile and a pinch of chagrin.

Somehow, he talked me on board, introduced me to Al and started issuing orders.

"Well, first we've got to put on this here thirty-pound brass propeller. Billy, hop over and spin it on the shaft, will ya?"

"Sure, George. I'll just … oh, never mind."

He and Al went forward and discussed the day's plan over a breakfast of beer and followed by, surprise…more beer. I stayed in the stern and contemplated how to accomplish the propeller mission. I truly needed to adapt the brains over brawn approach. That damn prop was heavy!

First, I grabbed a line to hang the dang thing overboard. I tied a bowline around the narrow base, lowered it, grabbed a mask sitting by the wheel and hopped over the side. I went straight to the bottom, which was flat, dredged limestone rock. The rope was a good idea, but I couldn't quite reach the prop shaft with the propeller. The boat was too far from the bottom. I went up for air and thought for a bit. Then back down I went and got into a crouch like a catcher with a prop instead of a mitt. I then jumped upward and just missed the shaft. One more time and I caught the prop shaft with the propeller and spun it on. All under the gaze of two big barracuda, who, of course, just love shiny objects.

I surfaced and asked George for the large propeller nut to secure it on the shaft. All I heard was a loud "shitfuck," which apparently was code for he'd forgotten it. I climbed on board and said, "Look, we plan to motor the whole way, so if we don't put it in reverse, the prop will stay on. Put it in reverse and it will spin right off, though." George said it was a good idea. At this point, Al said in a hushed tone that now would be a very good time to leave.

Al hurriedly started the engine and his attempt at an inconspicuous getaway was thwarted by the Pride's backfiring exhaust and ensuing mushroom cloud of black diesel smoke. We cast off and were motoring parallel to the dock when, surprise, surprise, the dockmaster appeared alongside. He was walking briskly in his starched khakis, clutching and waving a handful of colorful papers. The brisk walk evolved into a jog as the Pride picked up steam. He was yelling at Al for his forwarding address. Al pointed to his ears indicating he couldn't hear over of the Pride's ancient diesel, which was partially true. George was packing his precious beer on ice and I said a prayer to Poseidon and any other ocean deity that would take pity on an obviously daft fifteen-year-old.

The Ocean Reef channel had recently been dredged and was straight as an arrow but at the end took a dogleg left to sea. I was absentmindedly watching Al steer and realized he was going to miss the turn and run onto a flat. I yelled at Al to turn and he got flustered, pulling the gear shift into neutral and then reverse. Zing, off went the prop into deep water and then we slowly ran aground on a sandbar. Almost but not quite out of earshot of the eggplant-purple-faced dockmaster still yelling in his even sweatier stained khakis.

George deadpanned, "Well, this was a fun trip," and we all sat for a minute and pondered our next move. It appeared that as the sober and also proud owner of a thirteen foot Sunfish sailboat, I should take charge. We had no choice but to sail north without engine power. George and I jumped off the bow and managed to push the Pride off the flat. Then we hopped on and I took over the helm as Al still thought you could sail straight into the wind. Which totally made sense as his boat was made of crushed-up rock and dirt.

As we sailed north, Al and George made a serious dent in the beer. At one point, George mentioned there was a rocket base nearby connected to the Cuban Missile Crisis. His tales were so wild it was hard to tell fact from fiction.

We—I mean *I*—sailed north, trying to stay inside the loosely marked Hawk's Channel. As we—again I mean I—approached the entrance to Caesar Creek, I yelled forward to George and asked what the plan was. He yelled back, "Damn the fucking torpedoes, full goddamn speed ahead!"

Great. Captain Al and first mate George were drunk. Not just drunk, but Lee Marvin in *Cat Ballou* drunk. Foster Brooks drunk. Jim Morrison drunk. The fifteen-year-old boy who is now in charge of everything drunk.

I quickly ran through our … *my* … options. *They'll be no help. We must get there. This is our only shot. Pretend we're a vessel in distress and must dock and make repairs? Jeesh, with this tub we don't have to pretend. Looking at the chart, Caesar Creek had so many turns the Pride will never make it under sail alone.* The only hope was to use the boat's rubber dinghy to tow it in.

Somehow, I launched the dinghy from the stern davits, fired up its antique Seagull motor and maneuvered under the bow, where I had attached a towline. And so I started pulling the boat up the channel with the engine wide open. It was hairy, but the channel was well marked, and the current was with me. This was a blessing and a curse. Initially it enabled the dinghy to pull the concrete behemoth reluctantly westward. But as I approached the dock I realized all that momentum would cause the Pride to overshoot the dock and run hard aground. Really hard.

I slowed the motor to idle and as we passed the dock, I lassoed a big cleat with the dinghy's bow line. The Pride slid past me and then both boats rounded up into the current as the lines became taut and laid up right next to the dock. I jumped on the dock and tied up the Pride when George surfaced and blurrily said, "Need a hand, matey?"

Based on our research, this was the approximate site of Black Caesar's lair. My reverie was broken by the sound of a smallish bulldozer expanding the clearing. When the operator saw us, he stopped his rusty, faded yellow machine and walked over to the Pride. He had long jet-black hair much like the Grove hippies. He soon informed me that this was a private island and dock. And we must leave. I told him we were a vessel in distress and the law of the sea allowed us to stay until we were seaworthy again.

He started to argue, but then George stood up, shaded his eyes with his hand and said, "Charlie? Charlie Cypress? What the hell are you doing here? I thought you were running airboats for paleface Yankees."

"George? How the hell are ya?"

George jauntily replied, "Come aboard me shipwrecked pirate vessel and enjoy some grog." Apparently, adults spoke like pirates after twelve or so beers.

So, turns out George hired Charlie and some of his Miccosukee clan to airboat them around the Devil's Garden section of the Everglades in search of conquistador gold. When the airboat business was slow, Charlie did heavy equipment work for Richard Little. He hated destroying nature, but he also needed a paycheck.

After a few beers, some old stories and new lies, Charlie had to finish one last swath and then catch the transport boat back to Black Point. He said his goodbye and fired up the bulldozer. George and Al resumed drinking and I was trying to simultaneously formulate an anti-mosquito plan and also a ring search plan for the night. I was devising a long snorkel out of hose in my mind, so I could sleep underwater, when I heard a loud clink emanating from the front of the bulldozer. George heard it too and sobered up quick.

"Shit," we heard Charlie say, "something dinged my blade." George and I jogged over to stare at Charlie's nemesis. It was a large iron ring buried into the limestone rock. And it looked old.

The three of us stared at the corroded, embedded ring until George spoke. "That's it. That's Caesar's ring! Billy, we found it!!"

We jumped up and down like forty-niners who'd just struck gold. Charlie asked if we did the infamous brown acid. George and I stared at each other, and he gave me a look that said we could trust Charlie. So, George went on to tell the tale.

When he was done, Charlie said, "You guys need to take this. His Royal Dickness will grab it otherwise. He's been taking anything of interest."

"What else did he take?" George demanded.

"I'll tell you after we get this ring up."

George wanted to attach a chain to the ring, then have Charlie's blade lift it straight up and out of the ground. But Charlie said if it was threaded, it might break off at the ring. So, he found a steel pole in a debris pile, which he inserted horizontally through the ring. Then he used the tractor to spin the contraption counterclockwise, and sure enough, it began to rise out of the ground. I pictured an old buccaneer movie with the pirates turning the capstan windlass with a horn pipe playing to encourage them. Or the cat.

Once out of the ground, we all stared at it. It appeared to be part of an old anchor, but cut and modified. Man, those old pirates were clever.

George said, "Now what's this about Little taking other things?"

"Well," Charlie said, "he's furious about losing his land to the state. He thinks he was robbed of millions and he wants to get even. In a bad way. So whatever artifacts the crew finds, he's been moving to his house in the Grove."

"Anything interesting?"

"Sure. Tools, spears made with shark teeth. Pottery. Axes made from conch shell and a big limestone rock that was carved into the shape of a large sea turtle."

"What did you say?" George asked.

"Pottery, axes, couple of—"

"No, no. The turtle, the turtle. Is it still here? Can we see it?"

"Yeah, sure. Hop on."

So, we jumped on the back of the dozer and slowly clanked our way north up the Spite Road to Dick Little's base camp. There it was sitting on a crate about to be shipped. About three feet by three feet in size and covered deeply in the stains of time.

It was modern looking in its minimalist style. But it was clearly a sea turtle carved out of limestone.

When George saw the turtle, his jaw dropped. "What's wrong, George?"

"I've seen that turtle before." Charlie and I stared at each other, but George offered no more.

The transport boat's horn bellowed, and Charlie said he had to get on board. "Good luck, George. Nice to meet you, Billy." As he shook my hand, he said under his breath, "Keep an eye on George, will ya?"

I nodded yes and then George and I walked sullenly back down the Spite Trail. He was clearly lost in his own thoughts and I wasn't going to disturb him.

That night we sat on the boat and lit a fire nearby with palmetto root and wet grass, like Charlie suggested, to keep away the mosquitoes.

The next day we somehow got the wayward Pride to Dinner Key Marina. As we were departing, George told me to stop by Shangri-La in the morning. This was not wild-eyed, loquacious, pirate-treasure-hunting George. This was... *something is up* George.

Pirates, Indians, turtles. What does it all mean?

TEN

The next morning, I walked into George's kitchen, and he offered me coffee. No beer, no cigarette. Just coffee. Something was definitely amiss.

George was meditative and pensive, so I stayed silent until he was ready to talk. "Billy," he eventually said, "I'm sorry for all these old stories about pirates and treasure, but something's up. I can feel it in my soul. It's in the air. Maybe it's the south wind." That I understood. George and I both felt a south wind in Miami was a voodoo wind bringing in all kind of bad spirits and juju from the Caribbean.

"George, what's going on? Are you okay?"

"Yeah, yeah, I'm okay. I mean…I will be, but first I need to tell you about a trip I once made to Cuba.

"Back in the fifties I spent a lot of time on Grand Cayman Island. It was an up-and-coming scuba and tourist destination and it didn't hurt that the Heinekens were cheap. One night I was drinking greenies, as we called 'em, at the Blue Parrot in George Town with my buddies Abbott Bonden and Bob Soto. Abbott was a local who saw duppies when he was drunk, which, by the way, was all the time. He kept a rattle in his pocket and shook it sporadically to scare the bad ones away."

"What's a duppy?" I asked.

George looked at me incredulously, then to the left, then slowly right, and whispered, "They're like a Caymanian ghost, very real, don't like to be talked about. I think one or two followed me here!"

"Oh." That was all I could come up with, and George continued.

"Soto ran a fledgling scuba shop and had a taste for adventure, brown-eyed woman and Cuban cigars. He told us that earlier that day two guys had come into his shop who'd just returned from an underwater escapade on the northwest coast of Cuba. They were trying to sell their scuba gear to Bob, who ended up buying it for ten cents on the dollar."

"Why's that?" I interjected.

"The two guys heard a tale about a Spanish merchantman named the Valentina running aground in 1717, just outside of Havana. The info was based on a chart found on Blackbeard's *Adventure* when he was captured in 1718. The story goes that Blackbeard was based in the Bahamas and planned on shadowing the treasure fleet as it sailed northeast through the Strait of Florida with a plan to pick off any stragglers. Well, Blackbeard got lucky and right outside of Havana harbor he attacked and severely damaged the *Valentina*, which was accompanying the treasure fleet. This was a common practice as there's safety in numbers, but the heavily armed fleet can never risk rendering anything but minimal assistance. Their treasure cargo was simply too valuable to stop for a disabled merchantman. Blackbeard chased him eastward, then his own luck ran out."

"What happened?"

"His own rudder broke, and he lost sight of the prize. So, the divers in Bob's shop had info that the *Valentina* ran aground near Cayo Cabezos, Cuba. One was a real character. His name was Mel Fishman or something. Always saying 'today's the day.' Hope he didn't quit his day job. The pair spent several weeks looking for evidence of the Valentina but found nothing. Eventually they got spooked by the currents above and below the water. The political situation was dicey and they just wanted out. Bob said they were amateurs and covered only a quarter of the potential area.

"So, after a few more greenies—okay, a boatload—we developed a can't-miss plan to search the area thoroughly. Bob was in charge of underwater operations, I was in charge of travel arrangements and Abbott, international relations, booze, mixers and ice.

"Things were heating up in Cuba with Batista on the outs and Castro's rebel forces everywhere. We were concerned that American treasure hunters would elicit unwanted attention from both sides. So, using Caymanian passports, we flew in on a World War II DC-3 named the Yellowbird. She was, of course, painted bright yellow, but her engine cowlings were painted black. I asked the pilot, who apparently used dark rum as cologne, why, and he replied, 'To hide the oil leaks!' With that remark, we loaded our gear, boarded and rumbled down Owen Roberts's grass airfield and headed northwest to the land of cigars, mojitos and probably communism.

"We hired a local guide and stayed on the outskirts of a little fishing village called Morada Nueva, which meant New Abode. The local people were primarily fishermen and appeared to be of indigenous rather than Spanish. They were clearly at home on the sea and had never seen signs of our wreck, which was disconcerting. They stayed to themselves until they saw our scuba gear. They were certainly enthralled by it all. We even taught the mayor how to use the gear. We were concerned about revolutionary activity, but so far, these barrier islands with their limited population interested neither the right or the left.

"We dove for weeks and weeks, to no avail. Just a few small nineteenth-century craft that had been picked clean. Our enthusiasm was waning. Right before our reluctant departure, I came down ill. I think it was a brown recluse spider bite, but who knows? I had a hellacious fever and Bob and Abbott took me to the fishing village. There we were directed to the *enfermería* and a medic eventually showed up who passed for the region's doctor.

"They laid me on a cot and from there it got hazy. It's like I was seeing the world through one of those Vaseline lenses they filmed old actresses with. The 'doctor' looked at me, felt my pulse, felt my head, looked at my tongue and eventually announced, '*Hay una serpiente en su sangre.*'

"Then he issued rapid-fire orders and I passed out. When I awoke, the room was hot and the doctor was again looking into my face. Now he was clearer. He had a strong, intelligent face. Curious earlobe indentations. Like stars. Couldn't tell if they were man-made or genetic. He spoke Spanish, but a very peculiar version. I attended a lecture once on the Aztec culture—for the gold, of course—and I swear it sounded like that.

"After the doctor's intervention I recovered quickly, and I asked my friends what happened. They said the medic had fires lit around the exterior of the small building. Then the doctor rambled around town and eventually came back holding something.

"'What was it?' I asked.

"'Nothing. He was holding nothing. He went back in the building and had a fire built in front of the door. We shouted, 'What's happening?' and in Spanish his answer sounded like 'A lost soul has been returned.'

"We rested a few days and accepted the fact that we would not find the wooden bones of the *Valentina*. We gathered our gear, which by the way came from Bob's customers, and made our way to Havana airport.

"Upon our departure, many of the villagers

gathered and the *médico* presented each of us with a small hand-carved wooden turtle with an indigo-colored head. At the time we thought they were trinkets. Or a local tradition. A memento, perhaps. But there was something about them. In fact, on the way to the airport, Abbott proclaimed they had good juju.

"Castro's forces were in control of the airport, and treasure hunting and revolutions were like oil and water. We spied the Yellowbird on the far side of the runway. Her engines were idling, and I wondered if she'd run out of oil before gas. As we hustled our way onto the tarmac, we were intercepted by a young rebel soldier in faded and patched fatigues. He asked a lot of questions and nervously moved his battle-scarred rifle back and forth. At best we were in for a shakedown; at worst, a visit to jail and unpleasant questioning.

"At this point a barely sober Abbott addressed the young soldier, who was probably a *guajiro* from the countryside and had grown up immersed in all manner of superstitions. In perfect Spanish, Abbott inquired, '*Amigo*, how do you feel?'

"'*Fantástico. Viva la revolución! Por que?*'

"Abbott continued. 'I am surprised, *mi joven amigo*. I have the gift, you know. I am a santero and there is a duppy, a *demonio*, on your shoulder. A very nasty soul-eating demon.'

"The soldier looked at his right shoulder and Abbott motioned subtly with his head to indicate the other shoulder. The young rebel looked slowly to his left shoulder and began to grow visibly upset. Abbott started shaking his ever-present rattle in his pocket and Bob opened the valve on a scuba tank. The loud hissing sound sent the shaking man-boy over the edge. He started walking briskly away but shouted over the noise of the DC-3's oil-spouting engines, 'What do I do?'

"'Church, my son. Church. Confess your sins!'

"We eventually made it back to George Town without incident and, well … that's my Cuba story."

"Wow, George! I can't believe you were in the middle of a revolution. But what's this have to do with Black Caesar?"

George reached into his right pocket and handed me a beautiful, almost modernistic, wooden turtle with a blue head. "This is the turtle the médico gave me."

"Damn, George, it looks just like the Elliott Key turtle, but with a blue head."

"I agree. They're both loggerheads, which was an important food source in the sailing days. It's also carved from wood called lignum vitae. It only grows in the Florida Keys. A very unusual, very dense wood. It doesn't even float."

Then George reached into his left pocket and produced a replica of the first turtle.

"Where did that come from?"

"It was on my porch this morning when I went to get the newspaper."

I asked George what all of this meant.

"I wish I knew," George said. "I've gone as far as I can with this little adventure. And I'm getting tired. Real tired. There really may be a snake in my blood just like in Cuba."

As I hopped on my bike, George yelled out, "Hey, I need to go to Cayman next week. I need a driver. You in?"

"Heck yeah," I yelled back.

"Oh, and they drive on the wrong side of the road down there!"

That night I lay awake in my bed. It was like Christmas when you're young and too excited to sleep knowing something fabulous will happen soon. Black Caesar. Blackbeard. Cuban Indians. Blue-headed turtles made from dense Florida wood. Going to the Cayman Islands. I smiled as I fell asleep. *The adventure continues.*

ELEVEN

A few days went by and after one particularly brutal mowing session, George sauntered over and said, "Hey, I've got two tickets to a band playing Dinner Key Auditorium tonight. Why don't you ask Smoothie Girl?"

"I don't know," I said sheepishly. "She flirts with all the guys there. She'd never go out with me."

"Your loss," George said curtly.

Now as far as I could tell, George's taste in music centered around Sinatra, the Ray Conniff Singers and Elvis, so I was curious what band he had tickets to. "Who's playing?" I asked.

George said, "The Windows? The Doorways? Something like that. They were just on Ed Sullivan."

"*The Doors!* Are you kidding me? Yes, yes! I'll take them." I ran over to Noelle's shop and she was as excited as I was to see one of the biggest rock groups in the world. We agreed to meet in front of a new hotel called the Mutiny, which was right across the street from Dinner Key Auditorium.

As I left that evening, my mother asked where I was going. I replied that George had invited me to see a band.

"That's awfully nice of him," she said. I felt bad lying to her, but she still wished I slept in footy pajamas. And I was pretty sure if she knew anything about the Doors, she'd stop me from going.

We met on Bayshore Drive and eventually made it inside the concert, which was clearly oversold. The air was blue with aromatic smoke. Jim Morrison finally stumbled on stage at midnight and put on the greatest worst show in American rock history. Songs ended early or started in the middle, and he used every moment to yell diatribes about everything from LBJ to Flipper to McDonald's new Big Mac. But when the music was on, it was magical. "Light My Fire," "Riders on the Storm," and the haunting "The End," which sent shivers down my spine.

Noelle was happy, I was happy, ten thousand hippies were happy and then Morrison ruined it all. He was singing "Touch Me" when he thought it was a good idea to show his … um … stuff. And the cops, who were already on edge, went berserk. Jim was tackled, the crowd booed the "man," chairs were thrown and a small riot broke out.

I gave Noelle a look that said *Time to split this scene and fast.* We made our way briskly to the exit, but in the crush of the crowd we were separated. Before the concert, I'd suggested we should meet at the nearby Dinner Key dockmaster's office if that happened.

As I was jogging that way and keeping an eye

out for Noelle, a hippieish-looking guy with lots of beads bumped into me. Hard. He shoved a bag of marijuana in my hand and nervously said, "Hold this for me, brother man." And ran away.

Almost immediately, a sizable Miami cop with a tree stump for a neck was on me. He grabbed the bag, and heatedly said, "Where'd you get this?" As I was stammering a reply, he said, "You're under arrest!" and spun me violently around to handcuff me. My life was ruined in that instant. Goodbye Naval Academy, hello juvie. I was faint, trying to talk, but nothing came out.

Just then Noelle ran up and began shouting, "Officer, Officer, they're burning the flag!"

"Where?!" he demanded.

"In front of Pier Seven. They're going crazy. You've got to stop the commies."

The officer looked at me, said, "This is your lucky day," and took off running. As did we. In the opposite direction.

TWELVE

I was excited about our Cayman trip and met George at his house for the ride to the airport. After the obligatory offer of cigs and beer we hit the road, but as we passed Miami International Airport I asked where we were headed. "Opa Locka airport" was the reply. I had never been to its grounds, but I knew the Coast Guard's orange-and-white helicopters were based there.

We passed through security, which meant the gate was open, and pulled up next to an ancient, faded yellow aircraft with black engines. I got out of the Haze and stared open-mouthed at this Wright brothers reject.

George mistook my shocked face for aeronautical admiration. "Can you believe it?" he exclaimed. "We're flyin' in the ol' Yellowbird! What a beaut!"

I started to tell George that I would not be joining him today when the pilot stumbled down the boarding ladder and yelled, "George! George Henderson, you ol' sea dog. How the hell are ya?" Being downwind, his cologne appeared to be rum-based.

"Finer than frog hair. Cap'n Rick, say hello to young Bill. He's an explorer in training. Billy, meet Captain Richthofen. No one knows his real name, but he goes by Richthofen of late."

"Great to meet you, kid. Hey, got any limes on ya, George? I'm plumb out."

As if he'd expected the question, George promptly produced a couple from his pockets.

"Great, Cuba Libres on me!"

Captain Rick then lowered his tone and advised we should get a move on. Something about landing fees and avgas fuel bills. Stunned by all the craziness, I found myself on board in a rear-facing jump seat. As in the Yellowbird was way more of a supply plane than a passenger-accommodating one.

Cap'n Rick yelled back, "Smoke 'em if ya got 'em!" and then his antique Pratt and Whitney radials stubbornly came to life in a sputtering cloud of blue smoke followed by a rainbow-colored oily mist. Whew! I thought I'd have to go outside and pull on the propellers to get them started. Old-school like.

Just then, George, seated in the adjacent jump seat, leaned over and exclaimed, "Whew! Last time I flew her Cap'n Rick had me hand-start those bad boys! This is livin'!"

As we left the hangar area, I glanced out the window, and right on cue, here came an overweight guy in sweat-stained khakis running awkwardly towards us, waiving a handful of multicolored papers. I looked over at George and said, "Do any of your friends ever pay their bills?"

George smiled. "Aww, he's just sticking it to the man. Ya dig?"

We rumbled down the runway, chaotically left the ground with the grace of a pregnant albatross and headed south over the Straits of Florida. Climbing was a tad rough, but once we reached our cruise altitude I started to relax and enjoyed watching the ocean below. Soon the white-flecked ocean gave way to an island. A really big, green island.

"Hey, George, is that Jamaica?" I asked.

George looked out his window and said, "Nope, Cuba."

"Cuba! We can't fly over Cuba! They'll shoot us down! They have Russian fucking MiGs, man. Missiles too." I was now officially scared to death and, as the joke goes, wishing I'd worn brown pants.

George calmly said, "Well, that's probably true for a US-registered plane, but—"

"What the fuck is this?" I interrupted.

To which George calmly replied, "You have the privilege, kind sir, of flying in the Yellow Bird, the jewel of the Air Kazakhstan fleet. The Cubans love USSR satellite countries. Oh, and when we land, your name is Visily Nazarbayev. You don't speak English."

"What the motherfuckin' fuck is going on, George? I've got to be careful! I can't get arrested or go to jail. Especially in a foreign country. Traveling under an alias! I need to, I must get into the Academy." Just then I noticed the wooden boxes in the rear of the plane with unusual markings stenciled on the outside. "What the fuck are those, George?"

"Oh, nothing," was all he said. Before I could erupt again, George deadpanned, "C'mon, Billy I never went to college and look at me!" And then we both broke out laughing. I calmed down for a bit until Captain Rick walked back from the cockpit.

"We've got a problem, gents," he said.

I sarcastically replied, "Yeah, no one's flying the Air Marrakesh Express."

He looked at me indignantly. "Her name is Yellow Bird and we're on autopilot!"

"So, what's the problem?" George asked.

"We're out of rum! Ho ho. Just kidding." And he quickly produced a round of Cuba Libres.

I gave up and downed mine in one gulp and then noticed the captain wasn't wearing a belt. I turned over my shoulder to peer into the cockpit and, yep, there it was. Tied to the steering yoke. The leather belt autopilot.

I read once that old sailors never learned to swim. It put off the inevitable in case of a shipwreck. They thought it better to break into the spirit room and die drunk. So, I asked for another. And another.

I soon fell asleep and dreamed about Russian-built ground-to-air missiles on Cuban soil. I'm kidding. I was fifteen. I dreamed about Honey Ryder, Pussy Galore and me…in a menage à trois. At least I thought that was what it was called.

"Billy, Billy. We've landed."

"Billy's not here," I replied surly. "I'm Visily Gofuckyerself."

"You can be Billy again. Customs took the week off. It's the queen's birthday."

I'm not sure exactly how, but I soon found myself behind the wheel of a brightly colored Mini Moke, a euphemism for Little Donkey. Originally designed as a type of mini Jeep, it was also offered to the public and became the official clown car of the Caymans.

The ironic thing was George had brought me here to be his sober driver. And I was hammered like a steel drum. But way better off than George, who was sitting on the hood yelling "Damn the torpedoes," singing "Born Free" in a surprisingly melodic baritone and providing dramatic hand signal directions as I weaved on down the road to Sunset House. I couldn't remember if Caymanians drove on the right or left, so I split the difference. Right down the middle.

By the time we arrived, all that fresh air and ingested airborne insects sobered us up. Sunset House was a wood-framed house/hotel built on top of an iron shore that catered to scuba divers. There was beautiful reef diving right off their dock. George gave me a quick tour that ended on the dock. I pointed out to George that a diver left behind a real sweet setup. New mask, snorkel, jet fins, cherry-red tank, regulator, weight belt. "I'd kill for that rig," I said.

George looked at me. "No need, it's yours."

"Get outta here, George. I can't accept this and you certainly can't afford it."

"Well, perhaps that was true last week, but this week you're looking at the new tourism director of the Cayman Islands."

"Wow! That's great, George! I wondered why we were coming here."

"Put it on."

I gave him an awkward man hug and put on the gear James Bond style. You know, from a standing position, bend over, put your hands through the harness and toss the tank in the air so it lands squarely in your back. He said there was a reef a hundred yards to the west that I should check out.

I started swimming on the surface and was soon joined by George. In his skivvies and an old mask. Only George. We reached the reef and it was beautiful from the surface. I could even see large tarpon swimming on the bottom covered in their shiny, silver scales.

"Watch this," George said, the way that one kid on the playground would say before carrying out a death-defying feat. He dove straight down, thirty feet below, and disappeared into the reef.

I thought there must be a cave or tunnel that he was swimming through. So, I expected him to exit on the other side. One minute, two minutes. No George. Shit. I descended quickly to where I assumed the exit was. There was George. He was stuck. I handed him my reg and his blue face gained some color. With one last push he freed himself and we surfaced together.

"What happened? You scared the shit out of me."

"I think I put on some weight," he replied sheepishly.

"Well, that's not your only problem. You left you skivvies back there too!" So, we swam back to shore. Me in my shiny Jacques Cousteau wet dream scuba rig and a scraped-up, red-faced, white-assed George in his birthday suit rig.

That night we met Abbott Bonden and Bob Soto, George's Cuban expedition friends, at the Holiday Inn to celebrate George's recent appointment. It might not sound like much, but the beachfront Holiday Inn was the hot spot on the island and rocked to the island beat of the Barefoot Men and their really, really dirty songs. Possibly only rivaled by Big Dick and the Extenders in the Keys, but I'll save them for another time.

The conversation quickly turned to George's unique marketing strategy. He told his two longtime companions that the secret to marketing the Caymans was... not to market the Caymans!

"Genius," said Abbott. "Absolute genius."

"I don't know," said Bob.

George went on to explain. "If we market the hell out of our now-secluded and pristine scuba diving paradise, it will get overrun by pasty tourists and cruise ships. The reefs will get ruined. Then where would we be?"

Abbott exclaimed, "Your genius, sir, is only exceeded by your newfound ability to purchase alcoholic beverages for dear old friends. I propose a toast to the soon-to-be-knighted George Henderson."

"I don't know, George," was all Bob could say. "I don't think that's what the Chamber of Commerce had in mind."

Abbott reclaimed the conversation and said, "And kudos for the great practical joke."

Bob quickly responded with, "Yes, I'll agree on that. Another toast."

George looked puzzled. Then his two friends each placed a blue-headed turtle on the table

George and I were stunned. George said, "Where did you get those? I had nothing to do with it." The gravity on George's face told the duo he was not kidding.

Soto eventually said, "George, we each got one this morning. Opened the door and there they were. We thought you had someone put them there."

Well, the night evolved into a beer-and-rum-fueled bacchanal of legends, turtles, pirates, underwater recovery methods and, eventually, women. I even told them about Noelle, to which they gave me sage, learned advice.

"Get rid of her, plenty of fish in the sea. A week in Cali, Colombia, will cure your teenage lovesick blues."

"Nope, Rio's the place."

Before George could pipe in, Captain Rick sauntered up and said, "You're all wrong. This lad needs a week in Saigon. Trust me."

"Cap'n Rick," I slurred, "isn't there a war going on there?"

He slowly lit a Cuban cigar, smiled and replied, "I know a guy."

When we got back to the Sunset House my mind was spinning from rum. And legends.

The next day I literally dropped George off at the Chamber of Commerce. One of his many initiatives was to ask the local fishermen to stop cleaning their catch at North Sound. The remnants were attracting so many stingrays; he was afraid tourists would get stung. The Moke and I then headed to the turtle farm on the north end. It was a venture that was exploring the viability of raising sea turtles for food harvest. But they also gave tours and had an excellent research center.

I stayed and learned all I could about the maritime and onshore life of the beautiful creatures. At the end of the tour we were all offered a snack of fried turtle, which I declined. I was developing quite an affinity for sea turtles.

The next few days were a blur of scuba diving, island exploring, a trip to Hell (a real Caymanian town) and trying to hold my own while drinking with semiprofessional alcoholics. By the time we rolled up on the Yellow Bird, George's insane and chaotic world was starting to make sense. I hopped up the stairs, poked my head in the cockpit and loudly announced to Cap'n Rick, "Welcome aboard Air Hababastan! Call me Ishmael. I'll be your bartender and airborne mechanic for the flight."

Rick smiled and yelled over my shoulder to George. "Hey, your cynical protégé is growing on me. Who's got the limes?"

THIRTEEN

One of George's many abilities was to provide advice for the lovelorn. I'd been moping around over Noelle but didn't really know what the next step was. George's advice? Fuck it. Damn the torpedoes. Go over there and ask her out. Go see a movie. Take her to dinner. Have breakfast at Tiffany's. Get the girl, go on, ask her, don't be like me. I lost my love. Don't lose yours.

"George, I don't have any money. I give all my money you pay me to my mom. You know schoolteachers don't get paid in the summer."

"Hmm," George said. "Bring her to Shangri-La Saturday night. We'll have dinner. It'll be fun. I promise."

I'd known she couldn't turn down the Doors concert. But dinner at George's? After all my stories, that would be an easy no. Fuck it. Damn the torpedoes. I asked her and she said yes. Who knew?

I borrowed my mom's car and picked Noelle up at seven. She looked fantastic and I felt honored that she'd apparently spent so much time getting ready for our date. It was only later that I learned her mother had helped her iron her hair with a brown paper bag to prevent scorching. We chatted nervously about the weather, school and teachers. I was so nervous I thought I'd puke on the steering wheel and then she lit up a joint!

Uh-oh. The car was instantly full of aromatic smoke. I had never smoked pot before. Naval Academy candidates don't use hippie drugs. But I was three minutes from barfing, so I took a puff that she called a toke. Then she stared at me. She knew I was straight and was waiting for the obligatory coughing fit of first-time pot smokers. But I disappointed her and exhaled like Cheech. Or Chong. Not sure which one was the pot smoker. Spending quality time with George's ancient lawn mower and his endless Camels had probably conditioned me. After a bit I started to relax. Really, really relax.

Before I knew it, we were driving slowly up George's long ribbon driveway and I nonchalantly told her I'd built it.

"No way," she said skeptically.

"Yep … with a hatchet," I said, and she convulsed into a spasm of laughter. I thought that was a bit of an overreaction and I became embarrassed. Maybe her kind doesn't get their hands dirty for a paycheck, or in my case, beer and cigarettes. I replayed my last statement in my mind and then I began laughing hysterically.

I looked at her and we both said, "With a hatchet," and the laughing fit started again in unison.

I managed to steer us the last hundred feet without hitting anything and we were met by a sight I'll never forget till the day I die. I thought we were in the wrong place. Noelle looked at me a bit puzzled too. George had mowed, planted flowers everywhere, painted and even strung twinkly white lights from his gumbo-limbo trees. Shangri-La was no longer a ramshackle house/pier. It was a romantic restaurant hideaway.

As I shifted the car into park, an even more amazing sight appeared in the front doorway. George. Or what I thought was George. This George had slicked-back hair and a crisp white shirt, adorned with a black silk tie. All clad in a brand-new black suit. I quickly looked at his feet and, yep, shiny patent leather shoes instead of ninety-nine-cent flip-flops from the Army Navy store.

I was speechless, but George wasn't. He took several steps and opened Noelle's door. In the craziest over-the-top French accent, he announced, "Mahdam, welcoom … to Chez … Hen … dair … soon." Noelle eyed him curiously as he escorted her to a small outdoor table set under a tree with even more lights strung in it. There was a small vase on the table with two roses in it. He motioned for me to join and said, "Mousier. Oh Mousier, zee table is reddee."

I hadn't moved from the front of the car. My feet were frozen. He quickly came over and looked at me quizzically. I said under my breath, "What the hell are you doing? And when did you start speaking like Jacque Cousteau?"

The George I knew then spoke. "Trust me, go

join your date. And relax. I got this. Jeesh."

George saying "I got this" could be the most terrifying phrase on the planet. He said that as we headed out lobstering and definitely when we walked up to the Pride of the Hudson. I sat down and Noelle looked at me and I just shrugged. "This is so beautiful. So romantic. Do you smell the jasmine? I love it. Thank you for inviting me." And I felt her foot nudge my leg. Whoa, George was right. What I thought was embarrassing and ridiculous, Noelle was obviously enjoying!

As if our marijuana-fueled appetites weren't stimulated enough, we were downwind of George's aromatic kitchen. George walked up carrying two bottles of Perrier, a basket of warm homemade bread and a dish of butter pats carved into rose shapes. *Who is this guy?* I wondered.

Noelle was really loving all of this and smiled at George's absurd waiter act, so I started to relax. *Man*, I thought, *George really worked hard on all of this. How can I possibly repay him? I'll worry about that later. Tonight, I will simply be thankful and enjoy his crazy gift.*

Next, George walked out with a bowl of chilled shrimp. And two little baskets carved from lemons that held cocktail sauce.

"Wine, madame?"

"Yes, please."

It was watered-down Liebfraumilch, but we felt very adult by now. Next, George asked, "And how does madame like her Chateaubriand?"

"My what? Uh, medium, please."

"Very good. Most excellentay."

Noelle looked at me and whispered, "What's a Shadow Bree Ond?"

"Damned if I know, but I hope it's a big steak. I'm starving."

Sure enough, after George whisked the shrimp cocktail remains away, he brought out the biggest steak I'd ever seen. He sliced a portion for Noelle and then for me. He brought new wineglasses and this time served a watered-down sangria. But we didn't care. We were in another place. Perhaps Paris, even. Again, I felt Noelle's shoeless foot rub my leg.

George cleared our plates and asked, "Deezert, madame?"

By now we were both playing along with George's absurd waiter/chef character. Noelle twisted her hair into a silly thin mustache and asked, "What duzz zee chef recommend?"

George smiled. "Zee Key lime is talked about from Paree to Hialeee."

She said, "Two, please." Laughing, she added, "One for my man friend here also."

George smiled and exclaimed, "Oui, oui," twirled with a flourish and disappeared into his "bistro."

He next appeared with two perfectly chilled slices of Key lime pie, to which he added whipped cream from a pastry bag. And for a final embellishment, he shaved a lime rind onto the slices to add a bit of color to the authentic pale yellow produced by a true Key lime pie aficionado.

Noelle had never tasted real Key lime pie and her taste buds were overwhelmed. She once again started to thank me for a wonderful night when George wandered up. The real George. Tattered plaid button-down shirt, khaki shorts with an oil stain or two. He had his own pie and said, "Can I join you kids?"

Noelle jumped up and said, "Yes, please, Mr. Henderson."

"Call me George," he said and took a bite. "Damn, this is a good one." He finished his pie and said, "Well I'm going to visit some friends. I'll be back really late," he winked. "You two can go inside and watch TV if you like. Or play some records. I have the new Doorways album. Hey, before I go—Noelle, would you like to see the night-blooming jasmine? Billy's a Neanderthal and wouldn't appreciate it."

When they got to the sweet-smelling bush, George took Noelle's hand in his, but before he spoke, Noelle said, "I recognized you. You've been coming into the store ever since we opened. Ball cap that says 'Divers Do It Deeper.' Gray aviators. Mango banana smoothie. Hey, did you fix me and Billy up?"

George just smiled his Cheshire cat grin and simply said, "Billy is a special guy. One in a million. Smart as hell, hard worker, heart of gold. He's going to go far in this world. He's funny when he's not worried about that damn Academy."

Noelle replied, "I know, George. I know."

George continued, "And you're special too. You're wise beyond your years. I can feel it in my soul. So please look after him. I will be gone soon, and he needs someone like you." And with that he took off in his old Chevy jalopy.

FOURTEEN

The next day I headed over to George's to get an early start on mowing and to thank him again for an amazing night. Noelle had had the most wonderful time and I was pretty sure we were going steady.

George wasn't around, but he never locked his door, so I let myself in and made a pot of coffee. I sat down at what passed for a breakfast table and enjoyed the dark energizing drink. The indigo-headed turtles were on the table. I studied them. Compared them. Upside down. Front to back. And the dim glow of a lightbulb started to light in the back of my brain.

Just then George rolled up in a cloud of dust and hit most of his beat-up aluminium trash cans with the Haze. He half fell out, saw my bike and straightened up a bit. He followed the smell of coffee to the kitchen and slurred, "Top of the mornin' to you, Billy Boy." He was a mess. There were lipstick kisses all over his face and he smelled, I swear, of two different perfumes.

"George, I may have an idea. Drink this," I said as I shoved a hot cup of joe into his hand and pointed him to the shower. He emerged after a bit in a clean, tattered plaid shirt and torn khaki shorts. And a blue towel comically wrapped around his head.

Bam. *That's it!* The light bulb turned into the Fowey Rocks Lighthouse. Four gazillion kilosomethin's of illumination lighting up my head like a nuclear-powered jack-o-lantern.

"George. Wait here, I'll be back. And I'm stealing your car." I grabbed his keys, hit the gas and the unfortunate trash cans and left in a cloud of dust. It was all coming together, but I needed some peace and quiet. And books.

I pulled up to the library, which didn't open till noon, and it was only 10 a.m. But I saw Mr. Greene, the janitor, vacuuming and opened the front door a crack.

"Hello, William. You know we don't open till noon."

"I know Mr. Green, but it's an emergency!"

"A book emergency?"

"Yes, sir. Let me in and I'll take out all the trash for you right now."

"Well, I can't turn that down, now can I?"

I did my negotiated chores, then headed to the wooden file cabinet with the dreaded Dewey decimal cards. I wrote down the numbers I needed and eventually sat down at a table with books on Africa, Cuban geography, marine biology and South Florida history.

I'd always been a voracious reader, but now I was on fire. I flew through the pages, jotting notes on waste paper. African tribes and attire. Cuban coastlines. And Tequesta.

When I was done with my research, I had a

headache but was also giddy with happiness. First my night with Noelle, now this. I finally understood the word euphoria.

I thanked Mr. Green and drove quickly back to Shangri-La, narrowly missing the now-skittish garbage cans. George was sitting at the breakfast table nursing cold black coffee and he said, "Well, what was so hellfire important?"

"George, I don't know where to start, but when you came out with the towel on your head I thought of a turban. Here, look at the first turtle. See how the head isn't entirely blue? The area around the eyes isn't painted. Well, I thought it was just a missed brushstroke. But now look at the new turtle. Same missing stroke. It's not a coincidence and it's not a missing brushstroke. The pattern of the blue coloring was deliberate. It's the result of an indigo-dyed turban that stains!"

George looked at me and calmly said, "Billy, did you take the brown acid? That's some bad shit, *mi amigo*."

"No, George, be patient. There's a tribe in northwest Africa called the Tuareg that wears blue turbans that also cover their face. They're called the Blue People because the indigo dye stains their skin. Don't you see? The turtles have been painted to resemble the Tuareg. Caesar must have been a Tuareg."

"Kind of a stretch," George said. "I hope there's more."

"Yes, there is! The Cuban Indians that gave

you a loggerhead turtle figurine. Why that turtle? Cayo Cabezos has no beach. It's an iron shore. They couldn't possibly lay eggs there. Why would that turtle be important to them if they weren't indigenous?"

George said, "Ya got me."

"But there *are* loggerheads in the Keys! And in fact, Elliott Key has breeding grounds on the northeast side. Now for the wood. Like you said, it's very rare and only found in the Keys. There's more.

"In the library I found a transcript of a letter written by a Jesuit priest from Havana in 1725. He described the settlement of sixty Tequesta from the Keys to Cuba who were being pushed out of their lands and territory. They agreed to be transported if they converted to Christianity. The Tequestas were known for their fishing prowess, so to relocate and thrive on the Cuban coast a hundred miles away was not improbable!

"George, I believe that Black Caesar coexisted with at least one Tequesta on Elliott Key, and his Cuban descendants, or his ghost or maybe even a duppy are pointing us to Elliott Key!"

George was silent for a bit. "Damn, Billy. You are on to something. And not just Elliott. To the limestone turtle. They are pointing us to the turtle. What if the head was painted blue? It would be a fantastic clue, even the key to the whole legend. But it was so weathered you couldn't tell. We have to get our hands on that turtle!"

FIFTEEN

George said, "Well, no time like the present," so we hopped in the Purple Haze and drove to Richard Little's house in south Grove. We passed through canopies of fire-tipped poinciana trees introduced from Madagascar and enormous shade-producing banyan trees from India. So many beautiful things arrive in South Florida and thrive and enhance the environment and community. And then there are the human dregs that also flourish. People who only care about a buck. Wrapped in the blinding illusion of charitable contributions and camouflaged by the money they earn by contemptible means. These people flourish too. Richard Little was one of these invasive species.

As we neared the house, I gave George some last-minute advice.

"George," I said, "be diplomatic, okay? We may only have one shot at this. No insults. The past is the past. Let bygones be bygones. Love thy neighbor. Peace, love and happiness. Just like the hippies, okay? Swallow your pride. We've got to see that turtle!"

George stiffened. I had clearly insulted his eloquent oratorical skills. "I am commonly referred to as the U Thant of Coconut Grove. My patience and wisdom exhibited today will be sung by heralds throughout the realm for ages. I got this."

Uh-oh, I thought.

George drove up the long driveway to Little's ostentatious house. Reminded me what my friend Rob said about delivering pizzas. The longer the driveway, the shorter the tip.

George instructed me to stay in the Haze as he knocked on the front door with its garish gold leaf *L*. We could hear an ominous dog barking and we were both surprised when Little himself opened the door. He had people for those menial tasks. Up close he appeared shorter, fatter and balder. A big Doberman was at his side.

George had steeled himself to be diplomatic, to be the secretary-general of the United Nations. But a tiger can't change his stripes. Before Little could say a word, George said, "Well, if it isn't the dwarf King of Lilliput. I mean Islandia. Hmmm, I see the Metrecal isn't working."

Little replied, "I knew that was you trespassing on my island. And your ... your apprentice. I could have you both arrested."

"And do what? Put us in your cardboard box 'jail'? Get over yourself, Richard. We just want to see what you stole off the island."

"Sure, George whatever you want. Just get by Rommel here and the house is yours." With that, Little gave a silent signal to the muscular dog, who began growling. At the same moment, a landscaper fired up a chainsaw, which George casually turned to look at.

Little used the distraction to do what cowards

and losers do. He kicked George right in the balls, and George went down like the Hindenburg. I jumped out of the car and helped a gasping George to his feet. He was purple with rage; his fists were balled up, but he couldn't get a word out.

"C'mon, George, he's not worth it," I said.

Little then said, "Cat got your tongue, Georgie Porgie? That's for Miss Jane's house. You screwed me and now you're screwed. You and your beanpole friend." He then noted my pants and said, "Where's the flood, sonny?"

Now I was purple with rage. I walked over to Little, looked down and spat out, "You're a coward. A coward who hides behind money and mean dogs."

"Ooh, the boy speaks," Little replied contemptuously. Something inside me started to crack. It was a dam. A dam built of personal strength and resilience. A dam holding back confused teenage emotions. The crack widened from being fatherless. From being poor. From being an outcast of late. And from wanting something so badly, seeing it in sight and having it ripped away in a senseless instant. I braced myself for a moment, but the emotional current was too strong, and the dam crumbled under the torrent.

"Listen, you bald, pig-faced, turtle-dicked, chickenshit, son of a steaming pile of dog shit. George is more of a man than you'll ever be. Waving your gun around in your homemade police costume. You're a pathetic pussy. I'll bet your dad wishes he jerked off instead of creating an embarrassing piece of garbage like you. When you're dead and buried there will be a line around the block of people wanting to piss and shit on your grave. I'll be first, with three Ex-Lax in me. How about that, you weasel-eyed, bloated bag of pig crap?"

At this point he was a little speechless. George too. So I helped George into the Haze and shouted, "Hey, do you believe in duppies?"

"Huh?" he said.

"There's a soul-eating one on your left shoulder and his belly is full."

As I drove us home, George dryly said, "Well, that went well. At least we learned two things."

"What's that, George?"

"First, I need to stop cussing around you. And second, your mom's gonna kill me."

SIXTEEN

A few nights later I was reading *Chapman Piloting & Seamanship* assuming it was the official textbook of the Naval Academy. I heard the phone ring downstairs and ran for it before my mother answered it.

"Hello?"

"Hey, it's Noelle. What are you up to?"

"Well, I'm kind of studying. How are you?"

"Come over," she said. "I have something to show you. It's pirate related."

"I'd love to, but it's late."

Then she said please…real slow.

I rode the twenty blocks in three minutes. When she answered the door I nervously said, "Hi, what do you wanna show me?"

She said, "C'mon in. My folks went to Naples, so we have the house to ourselves." Hmmmm. I hadn't spent much time really alone with her. But my teenage hormones were percolating like a Maxwell House commercial. We went inside and I nervously began talking about the legend.

I updated her on the Little confrontation. She couldn't believe it, but who could? Truth can be stranger than fiction. We sat in silence for a bit. Each of us lost in a piece of the legend. I was obsessed with how to get a look at the turtle (maybe some other things too). After reaching my tenth turtle dead end, I asked, "What are you thinking about?"

"I was thinking about him."

"Him?"

"Caesar."

"Why?"

"Aren't you curious about the man?"

To this point I hadn't really considered him to be flesh and blood. He was like a figure in one of my history books. Someone to study their actions, their plans, their outcomes. Tangible things. Not their mindset.

Noelle could read my mind. And my face. She said, "You're such a guy. Don't you wonder what he was like?" My slow response answered for me.

"C'mon, Billy, he was a real person. He had feelings. Was he an average guy forced into piracy by circumstance? Or was he a bloodthirsty savage from birth? Or something in between? Did he have a wife and kids? Was he smart? What did he look like? He couldn't accomplish much on his own. What was his crew like? What was their camp like? What did they eat? Was the ring his idea? Perhaps someone on his crew was clever. We'll never know, but it's fun to think of the possibilities."

Again, my blank stare told her I hadn't considered any of these factors. She continued, "You should consider all aspects of his situation. Understanding his station in life and his motivations may lead you to the treasure."

She was right. I closed my eyes, and I was

transported to the hanging. "Can you imagine what he was thinking on the gallows?" I asked Noelle.

"Oh my God, how horrible. No, I can't."

"If it were me, I'd tell the whole world what I thought of them."

Noelle snuggled up a little closer to me. She said, "You work too hard and worry too much."

"I don't have much choice; I need to get into the Academy. I want to make something of myself. Chasing legends is fun, but not exactly a reliable source of income."

Noelle moved even closer to me on the couch and whispered in my ear, "Why don't you go on a different kind of treasure hunt?" Whoa!

Remember the Maxwell House coffee? Yeah, the pot was done and ready to pour.

I left Noelle's house around midnight and as I rode home I felt like I was being possessed. Hard to explain. A duppy? An ancient spirit, perhaps? Nope. The soul of Tom Jones was in me. I sang loudly and offkey into the night.

Whoa a whoa a whoa, she's a lady. Talkin' about that little lady, And the lady is mine!

My reverie was broken by a voice coming from a window, "Hey, kid, who sings that?"

I happily replied, "Tom Jones."

To which they loudly replied, "Then let him sing it! Asshole."

SEVENTEEN

We were at a standstill, but even with all our action the grass never sleeps. So, there I was one morning pushing the rusty two-cycle machine spewing blue exhaust when George wandered over with an iced tea and made the sign for "cut the engine."

"Billy. Summer is almost over, and you'll head back to school soon. I'd like to head over to Bimini, drink a few greenies, chow down on some conch salad. And cracked conch. Dive the Steps to Atlantis. How about it? Are ya up for one last adventure?"

"Sure, George, I'm in."

"Okay, let's head over Friday and come back Sunday."

"Sounds good."

That Friday Noelle dropped me off in her dad's car at Dinner Key Marina. George was already there with another guy and a brand-new twenty-one-foot boat. It was a new design called a center-console open fisherman.

George said, "Billy, say hello to Mr. Potter. This is hull number one of his new boat line called SeaCraft. Mark my word they are going to be a big hit. We're going to take this beauty for a three-day sea trial. So, let's try not to sink it." Mr. Potter and I laughed nervously and we soon cast off lines and headed to Bimini, forty-five miles to the east, with only the indigo waters of the Gulfstream separating us.

As we departed Dinner Key Marina, I noticed a new sailboat on the north end. She was about sixty feet in length, wood and named the *Mayan*. I later learned she was owned by David Crosby and the source of some of CSN's best songs. We headed east through Stiltsville and its wood-framed houses, passing our sentinels, the Cape Florida Lighthouse to the north and Fowey Rocks Lighthouse to the south, and then we entered the Gulfstream.

I told George to take the wheel and he declined. "George, I've only driven boats around the bay, I've never crossed an ocean."

"Ah, it's only water; steer ninety-five degrees and wake me when you see pine trees."

I was nervous for the first few miles, but the drone of the engine, the warmth of the sun and breeze on my face allowed me to relax and enjoy the beauty of the surrounding ocean. The sea was calm, and we flew through the deep blue water. Occasionally the boat would cause a school of flying fish to take flight. Amazing how far they could glide. After a while it seemed like a game of saltwater skipping stones. I watched frigate birds soar and wheel and acres of golden yellow Sargasso weed go by.

I was diligently observing the compass and after about ninety minutes I thought I saw a smudge on the horizon. Ten minutes later I could make out a line of tall pine trees.

"George, George, wake up. It's Bimini, I think. I hope."

"Okay, okay."

As we approached the shore, we passed several sport fishermen trolling for blue marlin, Hemingway's frequent quarry (aside from the bottom of any liquor-filled glass). Bimini had no extravagant channel markers like in the US, so George showed me how to line up the range markers on South Bimini to keep us in the channel from sea. It was a simple system. Two large colored squares on land, one in front of the other with the nearest one being shorter than the rear. When they were aligned, one on top of the other, then you were in the channel. Not aligned? Uh-oh. At this point, the water changed from the deep indigo of the Gulfstream to a thousand hues of aquamarine. It was beautiful, like riding through Lalique crystal. The water was truly crystal clear, or as Philip Wylie, author of the Crunch and Des stories, described it best, gin clear.

Before I knew it, we were tied up, stamped through customs and checked into the infamous Compleat Angler hotel. We were greeted by the hotel's proprietor, Helen, and she and George seemed to go way, way back.

"Helen," he said, "watch out for my young apprentice over there. He's a quick study and I'm worried I may be teaching him too much. Ha-ha."

Then he yelled to the bartender, "Hey, Bonefish, two clear-bottle Becks for me and Bonefish Billy here." Seems everyone in Alice Town was Bonefish somebody.

I spent most of the night looking at amazing and historic fishing pictures, many with Ernest Hemingway. I swear there was one with Hemingway and George in his twenties. But my head was getting crowded with wild stories, legends, etc. That night I ended up playing ring toss with the drunkest people I've ever seen. In hindsight I could have made a lot of money betting. I understood why George liked it here. Bimini was a fishing and diving paradise filled with unconventional people without a lot of rules.

The next day we headed south to look at the SS *Sapona*. Yup, undeniable proof that concrete boats do sink. After viewing the second concrete wreck in my life, we reversed course and headed back north. George taught me how to use bearings on land to find locations in the ocean. In this case he had compass bearings for the old Vanderbilt house and North End, which led us to George's steps.

We dove on them for a while and he was right. They certainly looked man-made as they disappeared into the abyss. To Atlantis? They gave me the heebie-jeebies. According to George a lot of strange things happen in these otherwise beautiful waters. "They don't call it the Devil's Triangle for nothing," he said. On the way in, he began a drunken story about an underwater city off the west coast of Cuba. But the sun and a few beers had an effect on me and I nodded off.

That night George ordered a feast of Bahamian delicacies. Cracked conch, grilled lobster, fried hogfish, rice and peas and guava duff for dessert. My growing frame could get used to this. That night I was beat from all the sun and sea, so I hit the sack early. Bonefish George partied all night with his island cronies. Almost like a farewell party.

~~~

The trip back to Miami began uneventfully. George's instructions were to steer WSW, which with the Stream's north current would put us right off Stiltsville in a couple of hours. And with that he pulled his wide-brimmed hat over his eyes, laid on one of the gear bags and fell fast asleep. The wind was south: a voodoo wind. George and I both believed a south wind brought up all kinds of spirits from the Caribbean. Some good but most bad. Despite my superstition I began to feel the rhythm of the small swells and confidently advanced the throttle.

I started to slide into a bit of a daydream. *Man, what a summer I've had. Adventures, crazy concerts, going steady with Noelle. I'm tan and a lot stronger. It's good to be alive. And not just in body but in spirit. My spirit is alive.* The song
~~~

"Feelin' Groovy" ran through my mind. Once again, the drone of the engine, the warmth of the sun and breeze on my face let me retreat from responsibilities on shore. Starting high school was kind of scary. The pressure to keep up grades and extracurriculars for the Academy was taxing too.

George was a trip. Passed out on a boat in the middle of the ocean, trusting me to get us home. I learned a lot from my wayward teacher. He really lived for the moment and didn't dwell on matters he had no control over. And right now, I had control of this sweet boat. There was always the chance of catching a few mahi-mahi, so I rigged up a spinning rod and a whole ballyhoo for bait.

After an hour, the south swell began to rise, and an unusually dark squall line appeared straight ahead. I held off waking George, but the pelting rain and small hail did the job for me. I heard The Doors song "Riders on the Storm" in my head. *Dum de dum, dum, dum.* The freezing rain hurt and visibility was soon almost zero. George woke up hazily and I told him what was going on. He said it might be bad for a bit and took over the helm.

Bad for a bit turned out to be the biggest understatement of our lives. The wind just kept rising and rising. Twenty knots, thirty knots, now fifty knots at least. And the rain was coming down in torrents. So hard and so fast we could hardly see past the bow of the boat. *Lord, please don't let us get run over by a freighter*, I thought.

The waves built up fast and were approaching

fifteen feet and growing. I was cold and scared. How could I be so happy twenty minutes ago and in so much danger now? The only thing holding me together was George's apparent confidence at the wheel. He seemed to relish our peril.

Now the lightning started. Crackling blasts that illuminated the marine fury around us. I couldn't begin to imagine what would happen if we were hit by a bolt. I glanced at the compass, which was spinning slowly in a circle. The ozone air was so charged with electrical energy even the compass's magnetic field was affected.

The huge waves we were taking on our beam were capable of broaching and capsizing us, so George adjusted course to take them a bit more on the port bow. The sun was now totally obscured. This new motion seemed safer and George developed a rhythm of advancing the throttle to climb the face of each wave then back off as we crested and ran down the back side. Too fast and we would punch through the base of the next wave, flood and capsize. Too slow and the current wave would push us backward and capsize.

I was terrified when George finally spoke. I wanted to hear "everything will be fine; this will all be over soon." Nope. George said, "Billy, you know we're inside the Devil's Triangle. I mean, bad stuff happens here. The juju *es muy malo* around here. Did I ever tell you the story about the six Navy airplanes lost right around here twenty years ago?"

He tried to continue the story, but I lost it. I yelled at George, "No more legends, okay? No more duppies! No more pirates and Steps to Atlantis. No more supernatural bullshit. I can't take it. Where'd they get you? Chasing empty dreams and now you're gonna get us both killed." I was physically and emotionally exhausted and scared to death. I could feel the thick sweat of fear seep out of my body.

My words had an awful effect on George, who stared morosely ahead but continued his lifesaving routine up and over each growing wave. It was bad enough that I'd spoken impertinently to him, but I'd disrespected his life. A private life that he'd shared with me. I felt terrible and I knew I couldn't take back the words that wounded him.

"George," I said, "I'm sorry. I didn't mean it, but I'm really scared. We could die out here. It's hell right now."

George calmly said, "Nobody's dying today; we just gotta keep the water out of the boat."

After five minutes he said, "Take the wheel. I'm starving. I'd kill for a Marcella's pizza right now. Let's see if we have any dry Bimini bread." The last thing I wanted was to take the wheel, but I copied George's boat-handling strategy and crested the next wave properly.

George grabbed the bread and held out a soggy hunk to me just when the boat took an errant wave on the port side. George lost his footing and slipped on the ballyhoo bait I'd left lying on the deck. His head hit the fiberglass deck with a thud that I heard over the thunder. Then the motor coughed and died. The only thing keeping us alive just sputtered to a halt. I grabbed George by the shoulders and yelled, "What do we do?"

His face was ashen gray, and his eyes were closed. He muttered, "Sea anc … ," and then lapsed into unconsciousness.

Shit. Fuck. This can't be happening! I don't want to die. The storm and sea state had become a dark violent animal. Spewing rain and foam like a wild water beast. And it was going to kill George and me. We were dead. If not this minute, then in five. *But I want my life back. I want Noelle. I want a future. I have unfinished business. So, no one dies today. At least not without a fight, goddammit.*

The boat's momentum carried us over the present wave, which passed under us like a locomotive. Only louder. "Sea an…?" Sea anchor? My mind was in overdrive. He'd once told me about a sea anchor. You can't anchor at sea… wait, it's like a drogue chute. Hung from the bow. Keeps you pointed into the wind.

We didn't have a sea anchor. Just two hundred feet of anchor line. Not enough drag though. I grabbed the fillet knife and moved quickly to the locker in the bow. I cut off the anchor and began tying and threading the loose end with anything I could find. Coolers, buckets, tackle boxes. Grab. Thread. Tie. Grab. Thread. Tie. I felt like I was out of my body. As if someone was guiding my hands.

The next wave turned us sideways and its successor would surely capsize us.

I tied the anchor back on and threw the whole mess overboard. We were moving so fast the line came taut instantly and the bow swung gratefully a few degrees south. The next wave almost broached us and in the next few seconds, miraculously, the bow pointed into the wind and the boat began taking the twenty-foot waves like we had an engine again.

I relaxed for a moment but realized the gear I'd tied on would break off soon. Not much could withstand the force and pressure of Mother Nature's rage right now. Once again, I recalled that old mariners never learned to swim as it just put off the inevitable. Was that what I'd just done for George and me? Put off the inevitable? *No! I must get George to a hospital. I owe him. I need him.*

His breathing was still shallow and his color gray. *I've got to get him to safety. I must get the engine running again. Why did it stop? It stopped when the rogue wave hit it. Why just then? Hell, it's just like a big lawn mower engine. Could it lose its prime just like Ol' Smokey? Did this violent bouncing slosh air into the gas line?*

I went to the stern, where the primer bulb was, and squeezed and squeezed. It was empty but began to fill with fuel. Just then there was a large cracking sound from the bow. The bow cleat ripped off, taking the makeshift sea anchor with it. The boat spun sideways as I turned the ignition. Once.

Twice. *Please, God.* We were going to broach any second. Third time. It caught! I headed down sea to escape the next mammoth wave that wanted to bury us.

I looked at George and he seemed worse. Still gray and his breathing was so shallow. The Coast Guard could send a helicopter from Opa Locka, but that was impossible in this weather. My only hope was to head west and hope for a break in the squall. The lightning had passed, and the compass seemed steadier. The wind and waves had shifted east about ten degrees, so I was able to plane off with the sea on our quarter.

It took two more hours, but eventually I saw Key Biscayne in the distance and raised Coast Guard Miami on the VHF. I decided to use Cape Florida Lighthouse as a visual reference and twenty minutes later there was an orange-and-white Sikorsky thundering overhead.

The pilot lowered a metal basket down with a man in it. He helped me load a limp George in and then off he went spinning crazily into the helicopter's belly. The basket was dropped again and the airman hopped in this time. A few feet off the deck he yelled, "How old are you, kid?"

"Fifteen."

"Damn. Well, your dad taught you well. You just came through a feeder band of a tropical storm! We'll take good care of him."

As I headed for the Dinner Key docks, I angrily thought my nonexistent dad had never done shit for me, but George had taught me more than I deserved.

EIGHTEEN

George wasn't allowed visitors initially, so I went to the VA the next day, but not before learning horrible news. Blood tests revealed George did have a snake in his blood. He'd had leukemia for quite some time and was somehow able to hide the fact. Cigarettes, beer and rum provided relief, but now nothing could stave off the inevitable.

A nurse led me to the ground-floor ward. Just as we walked in, a patient went into a nasty coughing spasm and my nurse escort immediately went to his aid. By now I had developed a sixth sense when it came to George, so I slowly scanned the large room. In the rear I saw a man at the far end, sneaking in through a window with three Marcela's pizza boxes. Street clothes over the absurd hospital garb! I looked out a nearby window and saw the taillights of a yellow cab pulling away. Of course, it was George. He spotted me and put his finger to his lips in a *shh* motion.

All I could do was smile. Frankly, by now I was accustomed to his antics. Oh, and I'm sure the whole floor was in on it, especially the man with the "nasty" cough. It was like a *Hogan's Heroes* episode, distracting Sergeant Schultz from his duty.

George's plan was a good one, except he'd forgotten one thing. There's nothing quite like the smell of a Marcella's sausage and onion pie. Nurse "Schultz" stood up and looked around the room, perplexed. Something was amiss, but just like a medical bloodhound, she followed the aroma right to George's bed. She looked under it and angrily grabbed the still-warm contraband. I heard the despondent and collective sigh of twenty men while the stern nurse said loudly, "What in the Sam Hill is going on here, Mr. Henderson?"

George indignantly replied, "What? We were hungry. Christ, we served our country, lady. Let us die with some decent food in our belly. Right, boys?"

"Right!" The boys roared their approval and I was loving it. So was George. Right to the end, George didn't just take the road less traveled; he blazed his own trail like a debauched and drunken Lewis and Clark expedition.

The boys and I were now focused intently on the standoff. Who would win this will of nerves? The stern nurse who'd dealt with belligerent, ill men all her life? Or the quixotic rebel with a cause? The garlicy aroma had created a communal, salivary hunger, but the "boys" were too infirm to do anything about it. They silently willed George to prevail. He just had to!

George initiated the action by peering past Nurse Schultz's shoulder and she turned to see what was happening behind her. But it was a ruse!

George sprang barefoot out of bed, grabbed the boxes and began running around the room, passing out slices as fast as he could. The old soldiers were teary-eyed with gratitude. George was running, dodging, spinning, leaping. It was a VA steeplechase with Nurse Schultz hot on his heels, but she was no match in her bulky white nurse shoes. At one point he put a head fake on her that left her holding air. Funniest thing I ever saw in my life. Until I realized he was doing all this with his lily-white old man ass hanging out of his pizza-stained hospital gown.

He ran by me, winked, shoved a slice in my hand and headed to his bed with two pieces left. I was literally doubled over and crying with laughter. And so was the ward. Best medicine the old soldiers had had in a long time. The nurse converged on her adversary, and they were both panting. Two warriors at the end of a good fight appreciating the will and guts of the other. George handed her a slice, she sneered weakly and as she walked out she surveyed the smiling men and said in an awful German accent, "I zaw nothing! Nothing!"

I sat down next to George's bed and he said wearily, "Did you see that? The nurse chasing me around the room with my ass hanging out … that was some funny shit, huh?"

I smiled and said, "Funniest thing I'd ever seen." We both were silent for a bit and then George began speaking in a hushed, serious tone.

One I was not accustomed to hearing from the devil-may-care George.

"We had a hell of summer, didn't we?"

"Yes, George, best summer of my life. There will never be another like it."

"Sure, there will. This was just a taste. There's so much more. Live, Billy…don't simply exist. Find the treasure. Literally or figuratively. Don't be a goddamn corporate robot. You're going to do something fantastic. I can feel it. By the way, would you mind doing a few things for me?" He handed me a sealed envelope that held something weighty. "There's a list in there and a couple of trinkets. Promise me you'll take care of it."

"I will. George. I promise."

"Okay. Now, what happened on the boat? Did you put together a sea anchor?"

"Yes."

"Damn good thinking. That saved our lives. Now this may sound a little weird, but, Billy, was there an Indian on the boat?"

"Huh?" I said. "George, are you high?"

"I know, I know it's crazy, but I saw him. A small man, old with dark leathery skin. He was dressed only in a deer skin. He was checking your knots on the anchor line. When the sea anchor went over, he stood rock solid and put his hands over his head and he seemed to implore the heavens. Then he talked to me and was gone. I didn't understand him, but I had heard the language before. It was the language the médico spoke over me in Cuba. What do you think it means?"

"I don't know, George. Maybe it's like the lost Navy squadron. It's not meant to be figured out."

"Hmm, maybe you're right. It's just crazy talk. I'm going to take a little nap if you don't mind. That pizza run took it out of me."

"Okay, George. I'll check in with you tomorrow." I stood up and walked away wiping the tears from my eyes. As I walked down the sterile, pine-scented corridors, Jim Morrison's maudlin lyrics echoed in my mind.

This is the end, beautiful friend…of our elaborate plans, the end

When I got to the car I opened the envelope. It contained a list. And two Spanish doubloons. The list read:

Billy,

Shangri-La is yours. There's a small mortgage on it but sell it and use the cash for college. The military can do without you. You were born to do remarkable things!

I'd like to be buried in a Jewish cemetery. Don't ask. Fine, they have good landscaping.

Find Caesar treasure. It's out there. I know it is. That fucker Little has the key. And piss on his grave for me, when he dies.

Here's two doubloons to carry with you. They'll remind you that treasure in some form is nearby. They were given to me by the Niedhauks.

Now for some advice: Never pay for a fuckin' mango. Ever!

Be good to your mom and don't cuss around her.

Don't ever order Key lime pie at a restaurant. Hang on to Noelle. She's special.

Remember the good things I showed you and forget the bad things. Please.

Thank you for helping me this summer. We came so close, but I will die a happy man knowing the legend didn't end with me. Vaya con Dios, mi amigo.

Love,
George

I sat in the car and cried like I'd never cried before.

In the morning, the hospital called. George was gone. And so was closest thing to a father I ever had.

~~~

That same night in Morada Nueva, the sleepy Cuban fishing village, an elderly doctor woke in a fever dream. He was both *caliente y frio*. His soul quivered. The snake in the crazy gringo's blood had won. He thought, *But as is everything, that is*
~~~

temporary. Perhaps I will see him again. And now the plan that was created by Capitano Caesar and Kalos must continue on. A promise of must not go unfulfilled.

NINETEEN

George's funeral was several days later and thank goodness Noelle went with me. I was full of emotions, never having experienced the death of a loved one. She literally gave me the strength to get through it. As we pulled into Lowenstein Memorial Gardens, Noelle said, "George was Jewish?"

"He wasn't," I replied. Before she could ask the obvious question, I informed her that was one of the items on George's list. He wanted to be buried in a Jewish cemetery. He thought the landscaping would be better. She started to laugh and so did I. Even after his death, his unconventional ways made us laugh.

George's funeral was something else. Of course, distant family flew in, but it was a real Grove affair. Hippies, politicians, two future rock stars (think Woodstock), a troupe of Hare Krishnas. It was wild. George knew way more people than I thought. I said a few sobbing words.

After the service I mingled half-heartedly with some of his friends. They were polite and many wanted to know how I knew him. I told them how I helped with projects but didn't let on about Caesar's legend. I was never wired for small talk, but I didn't want to go. I couldn't bear the thought of leaving George behind, helpless in the dirt.

Everlasting friends don't do that. They have your back. They stand guard. They protect, they stand watch, they don't fucking abandon. This maudlin train of thought brought more tears to my eyes.

Eventually I worked up the courage to leave, but first I walked over to George's grave and flower-covered headstone to say my final goodbye. I placed my shaking hand on his gravestone and inadvertently knocked off some of the flowers. And there, staring right at me, was a blue-headed turtle! Left for George. Or possibly me?

TWENTY

What happened next?

I'd love to tell you that I found the treasure, married Noelle and had a life that people dream about. Sadly, that wasn't the case.

The Summer of Love gave way to the '70s. The realities of a cold world set in. The Grove changed with developers moving in, building shopping centers and high-rises. Old bars steeped in history, like the Taurus, were knocked down, its Bohemian character paved under asphalt and concrete. Nixon, Watergate, the oil crisis, Three Mile Island.

I was forced to grow up. The world was falling apart and without the limestone turtle, my pirate legend dreams died a little every day… until the memory of George, Shangri-La, Noelle and the summer of '67 slowly faded away into a dusty, hidden spot in my mind.

But unknown to me, these memories were waiting patiently, just like the iron ring, to be rediscovered one day.

PART TWO

ONE

1716
Elliott Key, Florida

The small sloop eased into the swift current and noiselessly made its way seaward. The slightly intoxicated crew was grateful for the current's direction. Fighting an incoming tide would have made their piratical quest quite taxing. There was a half-moon directly above and the night air was humid as most were on these primeval islands. They rowed effortlessly through the twisting unnamed channel and breathed a communal sigh of relief as they left their mangrove shrouded refuge astern. Soon they felt the ocean breeze providing a respite from the ever-present drone and bite of mosquitoes and sandflies.

The pirate band was located on one of the northernmost of the Florida Keys. It was an ideal haven for their current occupation. Six miles east of the mainland, it offered quick access to sailing prizes and wrecks. But because of the long and twisting channel to sea, it was difficult for anything but the most maneuverable of sailing craft to navigate it. The pirates marked significant bends and turns with pieces of driftwood and, in true pirate fashion, scattered false ones about as well. The last approach, in fact, had to be skillfully navigated by lining up a large piece of driftwood with a palm tree onshore. To the west, the bay water was so skinny that only boats with shallow drafts could arrive via that route. These features all contributed to the pirate's sense of security.

Their quarry, the *North Star*, was a brigantine hard aground on the last reef, just offshore of their present sanctuary. The brig's grounding was aided by a beach bonfire that had led the *North Star*'s misguided sailors from their proper course. This rough band of seagoing rogues and renegades was led by a tall, broad-shouldered man taken from Africa years earlier. He was known as Black Caesar or simply Caesar. Ironically, the slaver he was captive in had run aground three leagues to the north, near present-day Key Biscayne, Florida. He was an imposing figure and it was rumored among the crew that he had been a king or a prince in his African homeland. It was clear he was a leader. Since being shipwrecked, he'd honed his newly learned craft and eventually flourished plundering vessels in South Florida waters.

Florida was the dominion of Spain during the early 1700s, but it was a lawless land and sea south of St. Augustine, the region's center of power. Spain, however, was well established in Cuba and there was increasing trade in the region, including the semiannual treasure ships' voyage to Spain and back. It was no coincidence that Caesar settled in this location as the heavily laden treasure ship's return voyage took them through the Straits of Florida now at his doorstep.

When the sea breeze hit their bearded faces, the patched sail was raised, and the craft and crew sped to the luckless vessel. The shipwrecked boat's crew had abandoned it and were in the process of escaping in two smaller boats. Caesar stood on the bow of his vessel and leaped the remaining three-foot gap separating the two boats, landing amidships on the port side. Just as his heavy black boots thudded down on the deck, the last of her former crew leaped from the starboard side onto his new and significantly smaller craft.

Caesar was immediately joined by Ulysses, his second-in-command and former sponge diver, then by the rest of his shipmates, who rapidly searched the boat. In addition to seeking the typical loot of pirates, they were in desperate need of provisions and appropriated all the galley held. Salt beef in casks, flour with weevils and all, spoiled cabbage and several small casks of rum, which were viewed lustily by the crew.

As Caesar stood on the gunwale about to depart, his head jerked at the sound of movement behind him. He jumped back into the vessel, hurled several empty barrels aside and found a boy left behind by the former crew. Caesar picked him up like a rag doll and bellowed, "A-spyin' on ol' Caesar, were ya?"

The boy was stunned by the pirate's intimidating presence, but also by his voice. He had never heard anything like it before. It was a form of seafaring English learned hard on the foredecks of British ships crisscrossing the globe. A linguist would observe that it sounded like the bastard offspring of Caesar's native West African dialect and cockney.

The boy managed to stammer, "N…n…no, Your Lordship. I was just scared. Please don't kill me."

"I ain't no Lordship, ya skinny ragamuffin!" thundered Caesar. And with that, he hurled the boy into the ocean as he seemingly had done so many times before.

Most mariners of the day could not swim or even float, as those skills simply put off the inevitable. And the boy was no exception. He fought the downward pull of his waterlogged clothes and managed to yell, "I can help, your lordship!" before a wave buried his head underwater. He managed to resurface and glubbed, "I'm a blacksmith, Your Honor. You need a blacksmith!"

As the boy resumed his descent, Caesar pondered that, in fact, he did need a blacksmith. Sailing vessels of the day were made of wood, but various iron, copper and brass pieces were essential to hold them together, and they weren't exactly near a port of call with chandleries. He also knew his simple crew didn't possess any artisan skills, unless debauchery and looting were considered.

"Ulysses," he roared, "fetch the boy from Mr. Jones' locker, if you please." Ulysses dove over and grabbed the limp boy by his collar. When they neared the boat's side, Caesar extended a rough-hewn oar to the boy, which he grabbed with all his limited strength. He was hauled aboard, and Caesar stared into the boy's eyes and asked doubtfully, "A real blacksmith, are ye?"

"Apprentice, sir. I'm a blacksmith appren—"

But Caesar once again hoisted him in the air and prepared to return him to the sea.

"Sire, sire," he pleaded. "Look at your mains'l hoops. They're cracked, broken, all buggered up. I can fix 'em or forge up new'uns. On Neptune's eyes, I swear."

Caesar held him there, high in the air, as he pondered the gutsy boy's fate. The young blacksmith's salvation was that he was quick-witted and sharp-eyed. Two characteristics Caesar admired and were practically nonexistent in his current shipmates.

He dropped the dripping boy to the deck and bellowed to the other pirates, "Welcome, young…now what be your name, lad? No matter. Smith be your name now. Welcome Smith aboard, lads—our new blacksmith."

The grateful boy was too elated to object to his new pirate nickname. For now, he simply pondered his luck and wondered what the future held in store for him.

When the last of the provisions were transferred, including the barrels of rum, indigo dye, also called blue gold due to its high value, and the tools of the boy's nascent trade, Smith's new, century-spanning voyage began.

TWO

Smith woke the next morning in a hammock, which he was accustomed to, just not on shore. The hammock was slung inside a ramshackle tent made from mildewed sailcloth. The interior space was large compared to his prior shipboard life. He rubbed his eyes, rolled out of the hammock, opened the tent flap tentatively and was greeted by a brilliant sun peeking over the mangrove trees with their spiderlike roots. His nose was also greeted by the sulfur smell of a swamp at low tide, mixed with a clean salt-filled breeze. Not unpleasant, but like nothing he had experienced before.

After his eyes adjusted to the glare, he took note of his surroundings. The pirate camp was in a clearing on the north side of a fast moving channel. A cut, if you will, between two islands. The channel was flowing eastward to the ocean and would reverse its course westward with the tide change. There was the pirate's sloop tied up to a ramshackle wharf and Smith noted how high the mast extended beyond the height of the mangrove canopy.

There were approximately ten tents and more campfires than he thought necessary. He ambled near the edge of the clearing and was instantly engulfed in a swarm of large black mosquitoes.

Startled at their number and ferocity, he ran back to the clearing and two pirates laughed as he flapped his arms wildly. The nearer pirate with more gum than teeth muttered, "Nasty buggers, they are. Drain you dry, they will! Stay in the clearing, matey, and near the fires and you'll soon grow use't to 'em."

One of Smith's ensuing chores was to add palmetto root with wet grass and leaves to the night fires to increase the mosquito-quelling smoke like a smudge pot. They dared not generate that much smoke during the day as they were, of course, outlaws and wanted by several nations.

A few pirates were milling about and Smith eyed Caesar across the clearing by the one of the campfires. He was seated on a log, carving on a stick, and motioned for the boy to come over. Smith walked over pensively, and Caesar put the scrimshaw-like carving down, inviting him to sit down. Smith did just that, less frightened, but also not exactly sure what to say. He had, after all, been abducted by pirates and taken to their lair. He wondered if he was going to be held for ransom and inwardly laughed at that nonsensical notion.

Caesar started the conversation. "Welcome to Elliott Key, young Smith. Coffee?"

Once again, the boy was enthralled by the man's odd accent and regal demeanor. *He's no heathen*, Smith thought, and he began to relax a bit.

"No, thankee, sire. I dare not."

Caesar replied, "And why's that, lad?"

"Well, your lordship, I was told it was the devil's brew."

Caesar roared a laugh. "Now who'd utter such nonsense? 'Tis a fine brew, me lad."

Smith replied, "Mrs. Garcia, sire. She was a seagoing mum to me."

Caesar's face tightened and Smith knew his next question would be coarse. "So where be your kin, lad?"

Smith's demeanor changed slightly. "Dead, sir. I barely remember them. I know we lived in Portsmouth. My da' was a blacksmith and I think me mum was a seamstress. But she died when I was a young 'un. Those were bad years and my da', he descended into and then perished of the drink. I was alone and hungry till Mrs. Garcia found me on the docks. She was the wife of a ship's cook. Since I knew a little about blacksmithing, she was able to get me a berth on their bark. And I've been sailing the sea ever since."

Inwardly, Caesar knew he had things in common with the boy. Knowing you will never see your homeland again is a thought that lingers in a dark place in your mind. "Well, boy," he said, "a lot of ocean has passed under our keels. And we are the better for it. Now trust ol' Caesar and taste this here devil's brew."

He handed Smith a wooden mug with rising steam. Smith sipped it and enjoyed its strong taste and energetic qualities. Smith's new apprenticeship had begun, with a pirate and his brew of roasted beans, both from Africa.

THREE

Caesar had the blacksmithing forge, anvil and bellows set up by Smith's musty tent. He earned his keep around the camp by mending broken swords and knives, fixing oarlocks and repairing gudgeons and pintles on the schooner's large rudder. He even laboriously constructed several small tridents for the pirates to attempt fishing with.

Trident fishing evolved to become a continual source of amusement for all involved. The sight of a band of pirates, wandering the knee-deep flats, stabbing wildly at anything that moved, would bring the others on shore to tears. Especially when a shipmate had the misfortune to be near a targeted fish or lobster. The result was typically a scream of pain and a one-footed hop, followed by colorful oaths such as "Damn you, One Nut, you shite-filled, three-penny doxie" that would make the devil blush. The better the curse, the greater the roaring laughter from shore. Despite the various foot injuries, the pirates were able to catch mangrove snappers, clawless lobsters and other hearty delicacies for their cooking fires. This new fare was a big improvement over the miniature deer, scrawny water birds and occasional turtle eggs they were used to.

Smith began to befriend the pirates, who were by nature a suspicious lot. All had wonderfully colorful nicknames. The aforementioned One Nut's was the result of standing behind a cannon just when the recoil hawser broke. Ulysses was Caesar's lieutenant, and his given name was Alexandros Papadopoulos. Hence Ulysses. He was a sponge diver from a Greek island that only he could pronounce. He was the only pirate that believed in hygiene but was extremely loyal to Caesar and felt a bond with Smith as he had saved him from the sea.

Stumps was missing a leg. And an arm. He moved about the pirate camp with a wild, undulating gait, but once on a deck he was as agile as an ape. Spanish Johnny was their on-again, off-again cook. He was from Havana and pressed from a Spanish vessel the year before when their prior cook had lost a quarrel over the age of a salt beef cask. Smith's new pirate clan began to accept him. All except one.

Paddy Nine Fingers was not happy with the boy's arrival as he'd lost his tent to the young interloper. He now slung his hammock with another fellow pirate but was still extremely offended. A seasoned pirate losing his berth to a skinny apprentice! One afternoon, soon after Smith's arrival, he walked by the boy's tent and found him furiously banging away with his skinny arms on a red-hot battered cutlass. Actually, Paddy stumbled more than walked by as he'd just traded a small sack of sugar for rum rations. After he downed much of the bottle, his resentment finally erupted.

"Think you're so ... crafty ... do ya, boy?" he slurred ominously. Smith did not hear the venomous words over his own clanging and banging. So, the drunk pirate went right up to him and shouted, "We should have let you drown ... you wee ... seagoing bastard. You b'aint no pirate. You canna even fight or protect yourself ... without the cap'n lookin' o'er ya."

The other pirates, drunk and sober alike, sauntered over to the rising commotion, Caesar included.

The pirate band truly did like the boy, but pirates being pirates, they also loved a fight. Fair or not. And this would not be a fair one. Paddy, although drunk, would beat the boy senseless. The pirates now looked for a response from Smith, who in turn looked at Caesar. Caesar could not intervene, for the boy would lose all respect among the men. Better for Smith to endure a proper beating. Smith noted Caesar's blank face and quickly summed up the situation. He needed his wits now more than ever.

Smith scanned his surroundings, surveyed the watching pirates, then calmly addressed his wobbly antagonist. "Paddy, you be too drunk, dim-witted and cowardly to fight a man like me. Go crawl back in yer bottle. In fact, matey, you'd need that there hammer to beat me with, you drunken sod." He then flexed his nonexistent biceps and let out a loud "Grrrrrr," and the watching pirates spit out their grog and roared with laughter! No matter the outcome, this was great entertainment for them.

Smith was inwardly scared to death, but this was his only escape path out of a perilous situation. The boy's invectives produced the desired result. Paddy was in a blind, drunk rage and he reached for the hammer. He grabbed it firmly with his five-fingered hand and immediately screamed with pain. Smith had taken the hammer out of the forge minutes earlier and it was no longer red hot, but hot enough to sear flesh. Paddy plunged his hand into a water barrel and cursed till he was blue. The pirates bellowed their approval of the "fight" and Caesar said loudly, "The boy has proved his point. Brains beat brawn. Unless a cannon is involved. Har har har. Now leave him be. Or face me. Your choice, gents. Now get some sweet oil for that drunken sot's hand."

Caesar's approval of the boy grew and over time, the buccaneer captain began to selectively reveal his life before piracy. At night, over coffee, sometimes dark rum, Caesar spoke about his past. He was from West Africa and had been taken by slavers on an infrequent visit to the coast. His people were fierce warriors as well as clever traders and oversaw numerous caravan routes.

Caesar enjoyed talking about his childhood and the adventures he'd gone on with his father. His father appeared to be an important man but had always found time to teach Caesar to ride and hunt and to instruct him on the ways of his tribe. Some of Caesar's favorite adventures were when he accompanied him traveling with caravans to exotic places and meeting other tribes. It was a great time in his life. His father sounded like a great man and teacher. When Smith would inquire about Caesar's adult life or family, he would change the subject and there would be, for an instant, an air of melancholy and longing.

Smith learned to stay away from those topics, so he in turn would relish the stories that Caesar told about his father and him. Smith began to imagine what it would be like to have been raised by a great, caring father. He respected Caesar immensely and wondered if the pirate could adopt him. He quickly dispelled the notion. A pirate with an adopted pirate son. Forsooth.

FOUR

One foggy morning Smith saw an apparition emerge from the heavily wooded north end and walk right into the camp. Smith knew these waters and the west Indies were said to be rife with duppies and jumbies, but he thought they were just tales. The phantom was, however, a small man, old with dark leathery skin. He was dressed only in a deerskin loincloth and carried a very large bow. There was nothing particularly unusual about his appearance, except Smith noticed his earlobes had starlike indentations. Perhaps it was a ritual? His movement and gait were economical and almost silent. The other pirates gave a slight wave, which the old man returned, and Caesar met him on the far side of the clearing, where they talked for an hour or so.

After the old man, who was obviously native to this land, vanished back into the woods, Smith approached Caesar and asked about him. "Aye, that be Methuselah, lad. You be my apprentice, so to speak, and I be his when it comes to livin' in this here paradise. He even has a name for it, but I'll be damned if I can pronounce it like him." By now Caesar knew Smith's inquisitive mind would not be satisfied unless he bared all about Methuselah.

So, he continued. "When some of those scurvy

devils over there and me first landed on this here island, we were soon met by ol' Methuselah. He was skin 'n' bones, but spry. He saved our lives. He showed us plants to eat, springs for water, how to keep the vicious skeeters away. Even took me on a trip one day south to Cayo de la Leña, where the hardwood grows. That wood is so dense it doesn't even float. And we rewarded him with knives and tools. One day he pointed to my bleedin' gums and skin and then led me to a small grove of little trees with small, yellow limes. The crew and I ate several a day, and within a week, we were pictures of health. On the occasion when we come across a prize with custard on board, we mix that sweet lime juice with it. Makes the best puddin' you ever had. Makes livin' here almost tolerable. Yep, lad. Without ol' Methuselah, I doubt we would have survived here.

"And don't let his age fool you. He knows wrecking, and if we aren't sharp, he may beat us to a wreck in his dugout canoe before us. Right happy he is diving in the ocean and pullin' up goods. Although he prefers tools to treasure, so we get along right well, har, har, har."

"What language does he speak?"

"Don't rightly know. I learnt some of it and he learnt some King's English."

"What do you two talk about?"

"Well at first, we mostly talked about how to survive here. But lately, me lad, we often talk about life. And even death. We talk about God, heaven, hell. Why are we here? At least that's what I think we are talking about, har, har.

"In Africa we learned from our elders around the campfire. So, I enjoy my chats with ol' Methuselah. And he wants to know about us. He knows people from the east are not good for him and his kind. In fact, many of his people have died and are being pushed south out of their homelands by tribes up north. I told him he should take people to Cuba, but that's a tremendous undertaking and they have no money for ship fare.

"So, we keep piratin' and Methuselah keeps a-goin.' He's a good man. Wise. He knows things he does. Sometimes I think he knows how the whole universe works."

FIVE

Smith was frequently assigned the position of lookout, not only to locate quarry, but also to prevent the pirates from being ambushed. One morning he observed a mast sailing on a course unusually inshore of most trade vessels. It was a six-gun sloop with a bow chaser, apparently sent from Havana to search out pirates attacking their trade.

Smith scurried down the tree and ran past the sleeping, drunken crew to Caesar's tent. "Sir, sir, wake up, your lordship, sir. There's a bleedin' boat flyin' Spanish colors, a-searchin' for us."

With that bit of knowledge, Caesar roused himself and then rallied his crew with shouting, cursing, a few well-placed kicks and one or two hammocks cut down along with their sleeping occupants. After a minute or two, Caesar managed to stir most of the pirates awake, but now they just stumbled around in two separate groups, in search of guidance.

Smith's clear head prevailed and he shouted in his prepubescent voice to one group. "You men release the port stays and wait for me orders." And to the second group, including Caesar, he ordered, "Release the main haulyard and heave right smartly to shore. Pull! Pull like your miserable thievin' lives depend on it."

Caesar's head was clear now and he understood Smith's plan. He broke away and headed to the vantage point of the lookout tree. He saw the boat approaching not less than a mile away and yelled back to his men. "You heard the lad. Heave like oxen, you pox-ridden, filthy swine."

At this point Smith joined the grunting and sweating men as they attempted to pull the mast downward and away from the cutter's vision. Unless the Spanish had absolute proof that a vessel was hidden in the mangroves, they would never risk trying to enter the shoaling, serpentine channel.

The pirates and Smith pulled and held their position until the vessel passed and then the ropes passed back through their bloody hands and the mast returned to its former height. They were safe. All due to the scrawny blacksmith.

Well, pirates don't need an excuse to celebrate. The boy endured Caesar's powerful blows on the back but inwardly enjoyed his shipmates' praise as they bellowed, "Now ain't he a pluck one, boys. Another grog for Smithy" and "Huzzah for the lad, huzzah for the blacksmith" and "Grog for the best blacksmith south of Saint Augustino."

The impromptu revelry went long into the night, and as Caesar and Smith went to their makeshift tents, Caesar slurred, "Good work, boy, fine work, laddie."

The next morning, a weary and aching Smith approached Caesar, whose drooping manner and bloodshot eyes made him a little less intimidating.

"Your lordship, I have an idea 'bout how to heave the mast down to avoid prying eyes. Especially if those Spanish buggers come creepin' 'round again."

Caesar listened intently and the two exchanged ideas all morning. By afternoon, the pirates were busy carrying out the captain's and blacksmith's plan. Smith's idea wasn't entirely unique. Sailors would undertake a similar process to clean a hull's bottom, called careening. Large trees were needed to anchor the lines to but were nonexistent on the island.

Smith's idea was to take a spare anchor and forge it so that its iron ring would be secured into the ground on shore. Then lines and block and tackle would connect the ring to the masthead. In this way the mast could be pulled easily downward and out of sight. When a quarry was spied, the process would be reversed and the pirates could quickly head to sea in search of plunder.

The plan was easier said than done. First the anchor's wooden stock was removed, then the flukes and arms were cut off. Now only the shank remained, which was heated white hot, then slowly twisted, effectively turning it into a large screw with a ring on the top.

Caesar came up with the next part of the plan that required a drill hole. He recalled how his people had dug water wells in Africa. Three long poles were used to create a tripod about fifteen feet high, from which a block was hung. A line was run through it and terminated in a cylindrical weight with a pointed end. A band of men could then pull back on the line and let go, letting gravity and iron do most of the work.

The only problem was, the northern Keys were formed by ancient reefs and therefore composed of limestone and not sand. But the determined crew, working in shifts, pulled and released all night and by morning they had a five-foot-deep hole with a three-inch diameter.

When the hole was complete, they placed the ring assembly into the hole, then inserted a long pole horizontally through the ring. With three pirates on each end, pushing in a circular motion, they effectively screwed the anchor shaft into the ground. It reminded them of raising anchor with a capstan, so they sang a sea shanty that made Smith blush and the pirates laugh.

The final step was to test the ring's holding ability. The pirates attached a block to the ring and then ran a line from the masthead to the block. This process was repeated once more. Then the pirates grabbed the standing end and pulled. With each heave the mast tipped downward and eventually it was level with the tree line. One of the pirates muttered, "Well, shiver me timbers—the damned thing worked."

That night there was once again typical pirate

revelry because they now had the dual advantage of surprise and being well hidden from capture.

SIX

Now that the pirate sloop could not be seen from miles away, the business of being a pirate picked up dramatically. When a potential prize was observed, the pirates would simply right the sloop and chase down their quarry before they realized they were prey. The pirate treasure hoard began to grow.

During this time Smith began to get a better understanding of his new pirate family. When he'd sailed with the Garcias, he had been taught that pirates were vicious seagoing highwaymen who killed for pleasure and stole anything from anyone. But as he became accustomed to them, he learned this was not the case. Assuredly they were not angels, but they hadn't grown up aspiring to be pirates. No, these men had been born on the fringe of society or eventually cast aside by it. Some had escaped debtor's prison, a particularly onerous punishment for failing to pay a small debt. Others avoided being pressed, and there were even one or two farmers whose crops collapsed. Then there were the simple. These poor souls could also be jailed and usually beaten, but here on Elliott Key they had a purpose and pirate brethren to look after them.

Again, they were no angels. They drank too

much and weren't shy about fighting. But they did have a code. A man's word was his bond. All shared in the work and the rewards. And most important of all, they looked out for each other. As no one else in the world would.

Caesar and Smith often spent evenings by one of the smoky campfires and talked. One night Smith asked Caesar, "Your Lordship, the night you took the *North Star*, would you really have left me to the sea?"

Caesar pondered his answer for a moment and then said, "No, matey, I wouldn't have. An ol' buccaneer I once shipped with taught me that fear and intimidation get you your prize before violence and killin'. And you did talk might quick. You should have seen your face, laddie." With that Caesar began to laugh, which grew into convulsive guffaws. "Well, lad," he said, "'tis a pirate's life for me and you! A toast, matey."

Caesar handed Smith a bottle of rum and Smith half-heartedly took a swig. Soon a warm glow enveloped him from the inside out. After a few more he stood up and proclaimed to all within earshot, "Ahoy, mates, a pirate's life is a damn good life." Those pirates witnessed a wobbly Smith fall backward over the log and then watched Caesar help the apprentice pirate to his tent.

~~~

Several times, Smith accompanied Caesar on
~~~

trips to Methuselah's camp. On this occasion he decided to pay him a solo visit to return an axe that he'd sharpened for the old man. Methuselah's camp was basically a clearing with a small thatch hut. In one corner there was a large limestone rock about two feet high and four feet wide and long. Methuselah was shaping it with a conch shell axe. It seemed important, but it was too early to tell what it was. Because neither spoke the other's language, they resorted to a form of sign language to communicate.

As Smith was leaving, he tripped over a root and exclaimed, *"Ay, Dios mío!"*

The Indian, who had started carving again, spun around and excitedly asked, *"Habla español?"*

Astonished Smith replied, *"Sí, sí."*

Methuselah asked Smith to sit down and they started a conversation in halted Spanish. Smith learned that Methuselah's name was Kalos and he'd learned Spanish from Jesuit missionaries who spent time at the mouth of the Mayaimi River. He was a cacique in his tribe—a chief. His tribe was dwindling in numbers from European-inflicted diseases and to tribes from the north invading their territory. They talked till dusk and then Smith hurried back to camp to tell Caesar the linguistic news.

When he arrived at camp, Smith searched out Caesar and told him about the visit. Caesar too was astonished and eventually asked Smith how he'd learned the Spanish.

"Why, Mr. and Mrs. Garcia, on board the *Dragonfly*. He was from Barcelona and I picked up a little." Thereafter Caesar would often bring Smith with him to converse with Kalos. The relationship between Kalos and Caesar began to flourish as each was impossibly curious about the other's culture and their past. In fact, Caesar's Spanish developed quickly and Smith was not needed as frequently to translate.

SEVEN

Several months after the construction of Smith's ring, the lookout observed a particularly slow-moving craft at sunset that was much larger than their customary fare. The time of year was right for the Spanish treasure fleet to leave Havana, pass near these waters, head east and sail their immensely valuable cargo to Spain.

Caesar roused the pirates, including Smith this time, as the prey was larger than usual. They soon had the sloop upright and headed seaward to investigate. As they closed in, they saw it was a Spanish merchantman named the *Valentina*. The boat's mast and sails were heavily damaged by cannon fire and she could barely make headway. Caesar sailed to the vessel's stern and pointed his large bow chaser cannon.

"Heave to or your rudder will be shot away and you'll never see your missus again," he shouted to the captain. "All we want is the gold. Heave to, matey. You have one minute."

The pirates were well practiced in their craft and relied on speed and surprise, as well as a ferocious presence, to take their prize. They'd even taken to wearing outlandish outfits designed to strike fear in their quarry. Stumps took it a step further and would howl and yell with a deer head, antlers and all, for a hat. The merchantman's captain knew he had no options and immediately headed into the wind. The pirates threw several grappling hooks and held fast. Caesar leaped aboard with two flintlock pistols drawn, quickly followed by his eager crew.

They were greeted by a wide-eyed mixture of passengers and crew and then by *Valentina*'s captain. Caesar and the captain walked to the vessel's stern and conversed in hushed tones. While the captains talked, the pirates and passengers milled about anxiously. Smith quickly befriended two sisters from France and soon discreetly disappeared from the deck. When the tête-à-tête was complete, *Valentina*'s commander addressed the occupants of his ship. "Captain Caesar and I have come to an accord. We will forfeit the Treasury's gold and silver and we can continue to Charleston for repairs. And he will allow all passengers and crew to retain their personal jewelry if they assisted with the 'transfer.'"

Now this led to an almost comical procession beginning in the lower levels of the merchantman, where bullion and ballast alike were stowed. Gentlemen and ladies in their finery, working side by side with pirates, all with the same goal in mind. To rid the boat of the troublesome treasure and continue their respective journeys—the merchantman to Charleston for repairs and the pirates to Elliott Key for rum. Lots of rum.

Although the cases were heavy, the pirates, crew and passengers made quick work of transferring the treasure. As they departed, Caesar swept his hat and made a leg to several of the ladies before hopping back aboard his craft. As he did, he noticed a mast in the southern distance. His first instinct was to cast off and pursue the potential prize, but his boat was almost awash with the weight of bullion.

"C'mon, lads. No use sticking around." And with that, they shoved off and the merchantman resumed its ungainly course north. Caesar did not seem to notice Smith sneaking aboard at the last minute smelling of two different perfumes.

At camp, the pirates couldn't believe their bounty. Old Sad Eyes played the hornpipe while several others danced. One Nut had pilfered a lady's bonnet and was dancing what resembled an eighteenth-century version of the cancan. Caesar was elated and, before enjoying a tot or five of rum, climbed the lookout tree and saw no sign of the mast. *Odd*, he thought. *Maybe she headed out to sea?* Caesar, who was normally pragmatic for a pirate, rejoined the festivities. Gold was a powerful distraction throughout history and tonight was no exception.

That night the revelry was unbound. But one by one the pirates dropped off to sleep and assuredly dreamed of treasure and perhaps Fiddler's Green.

The sun had just peeked above the horizon

when the sleeping pirates heard gunshots. They stumbled out of their tents half-dressed and unquestionably still drunk. There, standing by the fire, was a vision of the devil himself. Smith rubbed his eyes and observed that the demon was tall and thin but broad-shouldered. His dress was above that of a typical pirate. He had a six pistol bandolier, two of which were in his hands. But his beard and eyes seemed like they were aflame.

The fiery apparition spoke. "Morning, mateys. A fine mornin' it is. Join me an' my men for breakfast?" The apparition's crew then appeared in the clearing. Twenty at least, armed with pistols, cutlasses and one with a particularly large mallet.

The crew had fallen victim to Blackbeard the pirate. They were in good company. Contrary to common knowledge at the time, he rarely used force in his conquests, relying instead on his fearsome image to reduce his victims to malleable complacency to achieve the response he desired. A tactic that Caesar also understood.

Blackbeard eyed Caesar and said. "You must be the famous Black Caesar, the scourge of Florida, the blight of the Keys I hear about."

"And who may you be?" asked Caesar, already knowing the answer.

"Well, I be Edward Teach, captain of the *Queen Anne's Revenge*. My friends call me Blackbeard." He lit up a cheroot and smiled a Cheshire cat smile with a surprising number of white teeth.

"Now, mates, we have a problem," he continued. "I be chasing the *Valentina* since we wounded her with grape and cannon shot after she left Havana. She tried to lose us in the shallows off Cayo Cabezos, but then our steering cable broke and we had to heave to and make repairs. She somehow clawed her way through the shoals there and tried to make a run north for St. Augustine. We expected to catch her off Cayo Vizcayne, but lo and behold, some pirate scum took our prize before we reached her." When he said *pirate scum* the Elliott Key pirates bristled, but then again, they had been called much worse.

"So, who does the gold belong to? Your sloop with her sole bow chaser couldn't 'ave wounded her enough to take her. And perhaps we would have never found her if you hadn't claimed her yourself and unburdened her." Pirates on both sides saw the fairness of the argument.

"So, lads, I propose an even split. Half and half. We be like seagoin' partners. Deal?"

Caesar thought it over but knew this was the best outcome he could hope for. "Deal," he said, followed by a handshake including the time-honored spittle. The partnership of Blackbeard and Caesar had formally begun.

With business concluded, Blackbeard wanted to discuss the system for tilting the Elliott Key pirates' boat. He noted the extraordinary incline of the schooner and how it was seized to the ring. "Well, that's a clever contraption. Who thought that up?" he asked.

The pirates proudly produced Smith, who was reluctant to address the infamous Blackbeard. "C'mere, boy. Ol' Blackbeard's not as bad as people say. This be your idea?"

"Yes, sire. It's an ol' anchor I forged. But couldn't have done it without my shipmates."

"Well, boy, maybe you should sail with me…har har har."

Blackbeard and his band stayed several days on Elliott Key, sleeping on the shallow draft boat they'd used to surprise Black Caesar from the west. During this time, Blackbeard and Caesar had many conversations. Some public, some private. The result was that Blackbeard convinced Caesar to join him in the Carolinas to pursue more lucrative prizes. The general idea was that two pirate boats working in concert could cover a wider area and produce greater results, not to mention the increased intimidation factor.

The only problem was that Caesar's current sloop was too small to take on what Blackbeard had in mind. The solution was for Caesar and some of his men to sail to Nassau and purchase a frigate from Blackbeard that he'd recently relieved an English merchant of. The terms were fair and soon Caesar and his men were sailing on the *Queen Anne's Revenge* to Nassau, accompanied by Smith and Kalos.

EIGHT

As they approached Nassau, Caesar, Smith and Kalos went to the bow to get their first glimpse of the infamous city. It had changed hands often between the English, French and Spanish. But now it was a pirate city. No army, no government to speak of. Just a small town filled with various buildings, dwellings, a small fort and harbor full of pirate ships.

Many famous pirates made their home there, including Calico Jack Rackham, his wife, Anne Bonney, Charles Vane and Blackboard's mentor, Benjamin Hornigold. Blackbeard was perhaps the most famous and certainly the most enterprising. He understood that civilized nations viewed him like a tariff. If you sail in his waters, you pay a tax. He further realized if he killed and maimed at whim, then nations would send ships of the line to sink or capture him. Few ships or crews could best these enormous vessels filled with cannons and hundreds of sailors and marines. So, he walked a fine line between "taxation" and capital crimes.

The two captains, along with Smith and Kalos, were rowed to shore and arrived almost dry foot on the beach. As they began walking up a small dune to the town, Blackbeard took particular notice of Smith and Kalos.

"Hold on, mates," he exclaimed. "We can't have ya a-visitin' Nassau in those there clothes."

Smith was dressed in typical but threadbare sailor slops made from old sailcloth. Kalos—well, Kalos was just barely dressed. The two captains, on the other hand, were dressed in their pirate finery. Blackbeard's being tailored, and Caesar's borrowed from his prizes.

"Never mind, lads. Ol' Blackbeard will outfit you like a French frigate!"

As they walked along Nassau's main street, Smith and Kalos were dropped off at what served as a tailor in the pirate town. Before leaving, Caesar placed a small pouch of doubloons in Smith's hand. "Here ya go, lad. These are ya earnin's from the *Valentina*. Now don't be a-spendin' it all. Always keep a couple o' coins on yer person. 'Tis good luck, it be. Lets you know there is always treasure around. Har har." With that, the two captains renewed their course for Madame Marie's Boarding House and Tavern to satisfy their appetites.

When Smith emerged from the tailor shop, he was dressed in fashionable blue coat, ruffled shirt, breeches and shiny black boots. Kalos? Well, he'd refused to be dressed in eighteenth-century finery, but he did love his new tricorne hat. The two made an odd pair, but this was a pirate town and the inhabitants had seen far stranger sights.

The two found Blackbeard and Caesar holding drunken court at Madame Marie's, with old acquaintances, shipmates and even the infamous Anne Bonney. As they walked up, she was trying to convince Blackbeard she was born in Tír na nÓg, a mythical Irish land. As the argument reached a boiling point, they both drew knives and then immediately laughed heartily. Smith knew Kalos was uncomfortable in the smoky confines of the tavern, so they went to find a quieter shop for a meal.

They eventually found a food purveyor and enjoyed a good meal with grog. Smith had developed a small tolerance for the drink, but Kalos had not. The Tequesta produced a mild alcoholic beverage, but nothing compared to the strength of rum, even when watered down to grog. Well, Smith and Kalos got a little carried away, and before they knew it, the sun was setting. This was the time they were to meet Caesar at the beach to return to the *Queen Anne's Revenge*.

They bade the enabling proprietor good day and began stumbling to the beach. The first problem was that each was relying on the other to find their way. Kalos, who could navigate the Everglades and back bays by the stars, was useless in Nassau as all the buildings looked alike to him, so he relied on Smith. But to Smith, all the structures were spinning. So they just kept wandering around and telling funny stories to each other. Granted, some jokes weren't exactly understood by each other, but that just made them laugh harder.

At one point, Smith was retelling the story of his fight with Paddy Nine Fingers for the fifth time. Each repetition ended with Smith flexing his biceps and roaring "Grrrrrr" and then the two unsteady shipmates would erupt in laughter.

"What be so funny, gents?" The question was asked by one of four surly pirates who were blocking their way out of the dead-end alley they'd wandered into.

The boy switched from Spanish to English. "I was just telling my mate here about—" But he was cut off.

"What have we here, mates? A filthy Indian who speaks the spanney, and a skinny ragamuffin in fine clothes? Who are ya and what are ya doin' in Nassau?"

Smith, with great effort, slowly replied, "My name is Smith, sir. I'm……I'm the finest blacksmith in the Floridas and this here is Kalos. He is a king in his tribe."

Kalos, upon hearing his name, managed to make a crooked smile, then crumpled slowly to the ground and passed out.

The four pirates approached menacingly and Smith reached for his dagger. But it wasn't there. He'd left it at the tailor. The pirates' plan was to beat them, steal their clothes and purses and then press them onto their ship, the *Royal Fortune*.

Beatings and robberies weren't unheard of in the pirate capital, but pressing was a crime considered worse than murder. It was a form of slavery for ships who needed crew to haul on sheets and lines, turn the capstan and a myriad of other menial tasks. Many of the pirates had at one time been pressed by the British Navy for being in the wrong place at the wrong time. No notice to family or employers. Just a multiyear voyage in harsh and dangerous conditions.

Blackbeard and Caesar, having satisfied their gastronomical and carnal needs at Madame Marie's, found themselves walking and staggering along the same path that Smith and Kalos had taken. They both stumbled into the alley to relieve themselves of prodigious amounts of rum, wine and grog, but each sobered when they took in the scene at the rear of the dead-end backstreet.

Caesar put his hand on Teach's shoulder as if to say, *If I fail, shoot them.*

"What have we here?" Caesar boomed.

Smith yelled, "They're going to press us, Cap'n!"

Caesar began to advance on the four pirates. Not fast, not slow. Deliberate. Menacingly. The foursome turned on hearing his boot steps. They saw a single man approaching them with his cutlass drawn. Although he was rather large, what could one man do against four? They were aware of a second soul, but he was hidden in the shadows and currently posed no threat.

As Caesar began to close, his blood began to boil. He was back in Africa. The slavers were on the hunt. *Not today. No kin of mine is being taken today.*

His target, the closest pirate, said, "No need to cross blades, matey. These buggers just be a joining our crew for a bit." With that statement, the four all laughed together.

Caesar covered the few steps to pirate number one in an instant. The pirate was caught off guard at the speed and ferocity of the attacker. He slashed high for Caesar's head. Except Caesar moved like a cat for a big man and ducked easily under the man's sword, slicing his belly open from starboard to larboard. His blood, followed by his organs, spilled into a steaming mass on the dry alley dirt. The pirate fell open-mouthed to his knees, clutching his midsection, and Caesar continued his assault.

The second pirate, now considerably on guard, backed up slowly and waited for Caesar to attack. Caesar again dropped low and stabbed directly at the man's midsection. Pirate number two thought the crazed attacker was trying to cut off his manhood and was relieved when Caesar quickly withdrew. Until he looked down. Smith had honed Caesar's sword so sharp the pirate hadn't even felt his right femoral artery being severed. He dropped his sword and grabbed at the spurting wound. Then Caesar severed the other. Without stopping, Caesar continued on to pirate number three.

The third pirate possessed real swordcraft skills, and the alley began ringing with the sound of clashing steel, lit by the resultant sparks against an otherwise black sky. Each had a cutlass in one hand and a dagger in the other. They whirled and parried. Sweat flew in all directions and they both succeeded in slashing and cutting the other. Caesar managed to glance at Smith. The last pirate was behind him, holding him close.

Smith had never seen Caesar like this. There was a bloodlust in his eyes. The high-walled alley concentrated the rusty, iron smell of fresh blood, which in turn increased Caesar's seething rage. He amplified the speed and power of his attack and pirate number three couldn't keep up with the assault. It was a blood-spattered chess match and this pirate had two remaining moves left. The first was to raise his dagger arm to prevent Caesar's cutlass from striking his head. This only succeeded in losing him his forearm, which dropped to the alley to join his shipmate's bowels. His second move was equally ineffective, resulting in his head joining his severed limb on the ground.

The remaining pirate was holding Smith hostage with a battered flintlock pistol pressed hard against the boy's head. Caesar paused now, relying on his brains rather than his brawn. He eyed his adversary through slitted eyes, calculating how to kill him without harming Smith.

The leader, who had just watched his three mates slaughtered, announced with a trembling voice, "Now, matey, no more has to die here. Me and the boy, we'll just walk out this here alley and I'll be on my way."

Caesar responded slowly and deliberately. "That there boy be my son. And that sleeping old man is my best friend. And make no mistake, matey, you're gonna die in this here alley. But you can decide how. Hurt the boy and it will be a slow, terrible death. I swear this on my father's grave and his father before him."

Just then Blackbeard emerged from the shadows. The remaining pirate recognized him immediately and further knew that if the crazed attacker didn't kill him, then Blackbeard certainly would. His thoughts were addled, but he started walking cautiously to the entrance. Caesar was watching his movements the way a snake eyes its prey. Cold, unblinking and focused. Blackbeard reached for one of his pistols and this diverted number four's gaze. Caesar's sword arm flashed and the pirate involuntarily pulled the trigger.

Click. All heard the metallic sound of the pistol's hammer striking Caesar's blade instead of the spark-producing frizzen. Caesar's lightning-fast movement had prevented the pistol from firing. The pistol then fell to the ground, followed by the pirate's head, his face frozen eternally in bewilderment.

Caesar dusted off Smith and asked, "You all right, laddie? I'm sorry you had to see that."

Smith, who had witnessed violence in his short life, was visibly shaken. Nothing, however, could have prepared him for what he'd seen in that alley. "Thankee, Captain," he said slowly. "They were gonna take us. Why would they do that?"

"Don't rightly know. Some people are born with a black heart, and some learn it." Blackbeard then hoisted a limp Kalos over his shoulder and Caesar assisted a still-shaking Smith back to the *Queen Anne's Revenge* and the eventual safe harbor of Elliott Key.

NINE

A week after returning from Nassau, Smith was sound asleep in his hammock when a huge rough-hewn hand clamped over his mouth. Smith heard Caesar whisper, "Shh, laddie, shh. It's just ol' Caesar. Wake up, boy."

"What? Huh? Are we being attacked?" Smith was wide awake now and Caesar removed his hand.

"No, but Kalos has a surprise for us. And just us. Not for the drunken heathens." Caesar was smiling, and now Smith's endless curiosity triggered him to get dressed rapidly and they soon stepped out into the humid night air.

It was very late. Or very early. The moon was in the first quarter and Kalos was motioning to them silently from the north end of camp. When they joined him, Smith asked, "What's amiss?"

Kalos replied, "An amiga is visiting tonight. I haven't seen her in two years. Come, but be very quiet."

They tried to walk as silently as Kalos, which was an impossible task. They soon ended up on the island's sandy north beach. Kalos motioned for them to sit where the vegetation turned to sand. It was a beautiful night. A light wind onshore kept the bugs away, and the sound of the small waves lulled the boy momentarily back to sleep.

Kalos whispered, "Soon she comes. There! See her, my beautiful tortuga. Her name is Necahual, which means survivor." Caesar smiled, but Smith could see nothing. He squinted, but still nothing. He started to feel like the butt of a joke.

Caesar sensed his frustration and said, "See where I be pointing? Now look at the point from the corner of your eye. You will see it."

Smith did exactly that. Caesar's nighttime trick allowed him to see a shape, a head swimming towards them. He kept staring and eventually could see her directly. The largest turtle he had ever seen emerged from the slight surf and continued her swimming motion right up the beach. She maneuvered herself about halfway from the water's edge to where the three were sitting motionless.

No one had to be reminded of being silent as they were all quite enthralled now. The turtle began to dig a large hole with quick, jerky motions of her flippers. After twenty minutes or so she seemed satisfied and began to lay her eggs in the sandy nursery. This took some time, but eventually she reversed herself and covered the eggs with sand.

Only when she had completed her maternal task did Kalos walk down and sit next to her. It appeared to Caesar and Smith that he was having a real conversation. They "spoke" for fifteen more minutes and then she began heaving herself back to the sea.

Kalos rejoined the pirate and boy and said, "Few have witnessed so beautiful a sight. She is *magnífica*, no?"

Smith asked, "What did you talk about?"

"We talk about the ocean, the sky, storms, life. She always asks me to watch her babies, which I do gladly. They are like children to me, so I will confuse the raccoons and foxes and when the time comes, I will escort her offspring to the sea. It's a beautiful cycle, no?"

Smith noticed that Caesar was preoccupied and then his face slowly merged into a smile. As if he'd just discovered the solution to a problem. Before he could ask what Caesar was contemplating, the big man said, "Smith, I be staying with Kalos a bit. I have an idea I want to discuss with him. You head back to camp, but don't let those buggers know about the eggs or they'll be havin' 'em for breakfast. Har har."

TEN

Caesar was faced with a dilemma. He needed to travel north to rendezvous with Blackbeard, but he didn't want to sail with all the treasure they had accumulated. Since the nearby islands were made of limestone, there were no suitable hiding places for the treasure. With the pirates' bounty mounting, it was time to find a more secure place to hide it.

He had an idea, but he needed his crew to agree. It wasn't necessarily a democracy, but to ensure their loyalty, he involved them in important decisions. So, after a dinner of clawless lobsters and fish, a bit of grog and some custard pudding mixed with yellow lime juice, he addressed the pirates. "Shipmates, in a few days we leave Elliott Key and meet Blackbeard for a bit of plundering."

The loquacious men shouted, "Hear, hear!"

"But we must safeguard this here treasure," Caesar continued, and he pointed to the low-roofed rock house they used as the treasure cache. "And of course, half be yours."

Caesar had an equitable arrangement with the men. Again, to maintain loyalty. Half of the treasure belonged to the boat owner, which was Caesar, with the other half divided evenly among those that participated in raids.

"So, here's what I be proposin' while we be in

the Carolinas."

The pirates listened intently and eventually nodded their approval.

The seeds of Caesar's idea for a more secure treasure location had been planted when they were digging the "well" for Smith's ring. His first inclination was to drill holes on the island for the treasure with the percussion drill, but the islands were small and location opportunities sparse. So, his mind's eye wandered offshore. *What if we buried it in five fathoms of water? Take bearings. Place the bounty in small rum caskets with rings so a sponge diver could attach a line and retrieve when ready?* It didn't have to be a long-term solution as he planned on being back in a year or two and perhaps giving up the pirate trade. And if that didn't work out, well, he had made contingencies.

The next day the captain and Smith designed a raft with ample support for the three poles and stronger drill and larger weight attached. Then for the next week, the normally slumberous pirates worked hard building the raft and supports while young Smith banged and sweated over his anvil and forge, creating the needed iron pieces to make it all work.

While the pirates labored, Caesar, Ulysses and now Paddy Eight Fingers, having lost one to the red-hot hammer, surveyed suitable locations. They covered an area four miles north-northeast of the channel entrance, periodically throwing a lead line to determine the depth and bottom composition. After several hours, Caesar believed he had found a suitable site. They tossed the anchor overboard and made one last cast with the lead line.

Ulysses shouted, "Five fathom, white sand."

The captain next grabbed a small barrel with a piece of round glass in the bottom, to view the treasure's destination. He placed the barrel's glass just under the water and was satisfied. It was near a small reef with two small round-shaped corals with a brown swirly pattern. The reef was hard to see from the surface but would aid knowing eyes to the location. Lots of multicolored fish and heaps of those clawless lobsters walking around too. Next, Caesar used his rudimentary compass to take bearings from land, so they could return with the raft and treasure.

Caesar waited for a flat, calm day that appeared several days later. The pirates once again set off down the twisting channel, towing the raft to their new "vault." Consulting his bearings, Caesar eventually arrived at the spot and confirmed the location with his glass bottomed barrel.

When the holes were complete, the pirates finished the task by pushing the treasure-filled rum casks overboard in slings attached to the drill line. When over their respective holes, Ulysses would cut the sling and the casks would silently thud into place, creating a sand cloud that excited both the mutton snapper and endlessly curious hogfish. The final step was to cover the treasure-filled hole with a large rock brought from shore in a similar fashion. With the treasure finally secured, Caesar looked forward to a respite before heading north to rendezvous with Blackbeard…and his destiny.

ELEVEN

During this interlude, Smith and Kalos would often sit on the bank of the pirates' channel and quietly watch the wildlife. Caesar would join them sometimes, but of late, he seemed more interested in carving scrimshaw on the hardwood.

The humid salt marsh environment was foreign to a boy born in England's latitudes and so natural to a Tequesta whose people had lived here for an eternity. The most obvious physical feature was the channel itself. It was about a half-mile wide and even with that expanse, the water flowed swiftly, except four times a day, at slack tide, when the tide reversed its course. On an outgoing tide, the entire bay tried to escape its landed boundaries, only to return some six hours later.

It was this food-bearing current that brought all manner of avian and sea life. The birds were amazing in their number, color and variety. The fish equally so, although partially hidden by aquamarine water.

The higher altitudes were occupied by frigate birds, eagles, ospreys and pelicans, all of which had adapted various means of taking fish from the sea. The frigate relied on pelagic fish to chase their fare skyward, the eagle and osprey glided in on fish that strayed too close to the water's surface, and the pelican employed a bucket-like mouth to scoop up baitfish.

Other birds preferred wading on the flats in search of their food. Majestic grey herons, white egrets, orange-pink flamingos and white-pink spoonbills would silently wade through shallow water in their search for food. The spoonbill was aptly named, as it appeared to eat the primordial ooze with its utensil of a bill.

The dark-colored anhinga was unsure if it was a bird or a fish. It could hunt and spearfish underwater and fly as well as its brethren, but it needed an interlude between the two environs to air-dry its wings. This was Smith's favorite bird as it lived between two worlds much like he did.

Under the water there were an equal number of creatures. Shoals of bait fish pursued by jacks, snappers and tarpon, who were seemingly covered in shiny pieces of eight. The tarpon, in turn, were pursued by hammer-headed sharks who truly were the dominant creatures in the channel—aside from the pirates.

During cooler months, lumbering manatees of all sizes would swim through the pass. Kalos said they were delicious, but the pirates begged him not to kill the friendly creatures. Pirates and most mariners, being a highly superstitious lot, felt they were good luck to have around. Even the most hardened of the pirate band could be seen feeding the giants some of their cabbage leftovers.

Of all the creatures in the cut, Kalos was

especially fond of the sea turtle. Like the anhinga, they seemed content in the water or on land. His people had many legends about them, but Smith's favorite involved a turtle king that could invite you to visit a city under the sea. Kalos said the Lucayans to the east also believed this.

It truly was a beautiful and magical place. Smith felt like if there was a heaven, then Elliott Key was it.

TWELVE

As the pirates were making last-minute preparations for the voyage northward, Caesar became ill. He had been unknowingly bitten by a venomous spider while helping to collect wood for the raft. It went unnoticed amongst all the other bites they suffered, until a red circle appeared around the bite, and he came down with a high fever and tremors. As he lay in his tent, delusional with venom and infection, the pirates used all their medical knowledge, including the obligatory bloodletting by the crew's barber, but to no avail. As Caesar worsened, Smith went to get Kalos. Perhaps his knowledge of natural medicine could save Caesar as the fever was out of control and he was in danger of dying.

Kalos arrived with Smith and brought only a small rattle made from a gourd. He entered Caesar's tent and looked at his friend and the spider bite. "*Muy malo*," he said, then instructed the pirates to build campfires all around the tent, except at the entrance. He then plunged into the woods with his rattle and a torch. He spent thirty minutes yelling and shaking his rattle. If the pirates had not known of his skills and help keeping the captain and crew alive in the early days on the island, they would have thought he was *loco* as they were all learning Spanish here and there.

Eventually Kalos returned, acting as if he was holding something in his arms, like a squirming infant. But the pirates saw nothing. Kalos went into the tent with Smith and told the pirates to quickly start a final fire in front of the tent entrance.

Kalos and Smith stayed with Caesar through the night. Around midnight Caesar awoke in a sweaty fever dream and saw Kalos hovering among him, speaking Tequesta. Caesar collapsed, assuring himself that he was in hell but smiling as he'd thought it would be hotter.

In the morning the fever broke, and Caesar asked for water. After a few sips he said to Kalos, "I was dead, mate. How'd you bring me back?"

Kalos knew he wouldn't understand, but he tried to explain through Smith anyway. "One of your souls left you—your shadow soul. I went into the woods and brought it back and then surrounded you with fire, so it could not leave. You will be all right now."

Kalos started to leave, but Caesar sat up and weakly said, "Thankee, Kalos, thankee. I had one foot in the grave. Smith, be a good lad and hand me that there cloth." Caesar presented the indigo blue cloth to Kalos and said, "This is my tagelmust. It's very important in my tribe. Wrap it around your head and face and it will protect you from evil. I want you to have it. Beware, though, the indigo dye will rub off on your skin. In fact, my people in Africa are called the Blue People. Har, har, har.

Picture Kalos with a blue head!"

Kalos had seen the cloth before and secretly coveted it. The only blue he had ever seen was in the sky and ocean, and now it was on cloth. Powerful medicine. Kalos accepted the valued gift, wrapped it around his head, paraded through camp and proudly returned north to his own encampment.

~~~

With Caesar fully recovered, it was time for the captain and crew to head north and rendezvous with Blackbeard. The pirates hurried back and forth, loading their necessities on board the new *Salacia*, including the all-important rum casks. Many supplies were left behind, but it was understood that Kalos could take anything he needed.

Kalos was there to see the band of pirates off, proudly wearing his blue turban. The pirates good-naturedly teased him, but Kalos took great pride in this headgear. Possibly because it had been given in the face of life and death. An event that Kalos felt privileged to take part in.

Kalos had grown extremely fond of his pirate family, and they weren't used to seeing the old Indian being so emotional. In fact, he made a point to give each one a brief embrace and said a small Tequesta phrase, which they all believed to be good luck.
~~~

Kalos lingered with Smith for a bit and then only the old Indian and Caesar remained on the beach. They were deeply engrossed in conversation when Ulysses yelled out, "We're a-missin' the tide, Cap'n!"

Caesar good-naturedly yelled back, "Stow your gob, you spineless sponger!" But he did end his conversation with Kalos, which concluded with Caesar handing him the scrimshaw stick he carved nightly.

Caesar jumped aboard and, holding on to the stays, barked orders to depart and waved to his old friend. Kalos, in turn, stood on the beach forlornly waving goodbye to his island companions.

"*Vayan con Dios, mis amigos*," he whispered to the wind.

THIRTEEN

Caesar and his crew sailed northward to the Carolinas using the Gulfstream like a never-ending favorable tide. They avoided all manner of shipping until they reached the rendezvous point in the spring of 1718. Once there, they immediately joined Blackbeard and the *Queen Anne's Revenge*.

From their respective decks, Blackbeard and Caesar terrorized the shipping of the mid-Atlantic states all spring and summer. Smith was allowed on some of these missions, and he closely watched how Blackbeard operated. He truly did rely more on threat and speed rather than using blunt force and violence. It was almost like a business transaction with buccaneer theatrics. However, the crew were always ready to satisfy their bloodlust with cannons, muskets and swords.

By summer's end the marauding pair had amassed a fortune in treasure, at which point Blackbeard inexplicably curtailed his pirate activities. Then, as if to add an exclamation point to the cessation, he also ran the *Queen Anne's Revenge* up on a sandbar, taking her out action. Caesar obviously was concerned with this turn of events, but Blackbeard was evasive when pressed for a reason. The word in the dark corners of the docks and wharfs up and down the coast was that

Blackbeard had received a royal pardon in exchange for terminating the business of being a pirate. Caesar, in turn, used this time to effect repairs, while Smith was kept busy blacksmithing.

One cold November morning, a small cutter arrived with a dinner invitation for Caesar and Smith aboard Blackbeard's new smaller vessel, the *Adventure*. Caesar confided to Smith that he hoped they would learn Blackbeard's plans for the future, given his unusual actions of late.

After a reluctant but needed hot bath, Caesar and Smith were rowed noisily toward Blackbeard's new flagship, in their Bristol fashion jolly boat. Their destination was anchored at the end of a long channel inside of Ocracoke Island, one of the Carolinas' barrier islands. An anchorage more suited for a merchantman than a wily pirate that favored multiple escape routes should the situation arise. By now it was well known that Blackbeard had, in fact, received a pardon for his past transgressions and had begun to transition from the "Scourge of the Seas" to "Gentleman Teach." It was also well known that he occasionally reneged on this royal arrangement. When the jolly boat came up alongside the *Adventure*, the occupants shed their boat cloaks and clambered up the boat's sides, hindered by their new finery.

Blackbeard was there to greet them in his customary black knee-high boots, long silk coat and wide black hat. And his namesake beard was no longer braided in pigtails but looked almost gentlemanly. "Ahoy, me mates! Welcome aboard. Sluice your gob with some rum? Grog? Whiskey? Ale for the boy?"

Pirate pleasantries were exchanged, and Smith noted the small crew and even smaller number of cannons. This was ironic, as the *Queen Anne's Revenge* positively bristled with both. The deck was brightly lit with oil lanterns and candles, which was not only festive but a display of Blackbeard's prosperity as well. Smith thought every sailor knew that light hindered one's night vision. *'Tis true*, Smith thought. *Ol' Blackbeard truly must be giving up the pirate life.*

Blackbeard gave a quick tour and then they descended below to a large boardroom where an elegant feast had been prepared. Neither Caesar nor Smith had ever seen so much food in one setting: mutton, venison, turkey, cheeses, soups and an endless supply of wine, rum and syllabub. And several puddings for dessert.

There were three other men seated at the large table, and as introductions were made, it was clear they did not relish a boy at the meal. Their attire was typical of traders and Smith didn't like the cut of their jibs either.

Blackbeard noted the strain and said authoritatively, "Aye, he be but a boy, but this laddie has earned a seat at this here table. Sharpest mind and best blacksmith from Charleston to Havana, he is. So, drink up, gents. A toast to the fair *Adventure*, perhaps?" Glasses were raised and the meal began in earnest.

As appetites were satiated, the talk turned to business, colonial politics and women. Smith knew it would be civil now to take a turn on deck. He excused himself and went topside to enjoy the fresh salt air. He made small conversation with the two crewmen on watch and was not impressed with their vigilance. The deck was still brightly lit, and once again he reflected on this. Vision was so important to pirates that many pierced their ears and wore gold hoops in the belief this improved their eyesight. Eventually the taciturn crew returned to the stern, where a small brazier provided warmth, and Smith walked forward to the bow and sat on the small capstan.

His mind wandered to all the exploits he'd been a party to. A poor orphan boy from Portsmouth captured by Caesar, seeing and handling treasure of incalculable value, observing ancient Indians and now a king's meal with Blackbeard the Pirate. If he told such a tale in some quarters he'd be beaten for lying. His mind continued to wander, but to the west he thought he saw a tall mast. Then it was gone. He rubbed his eyes. No mast. He squinted, he stared, but no mast.

Then he remembered the trick Caesar had taught him back on the beach. Look slightly to the left or right of something you can scarcely see in the dark. The object will become clearer looking at it from the corner of your eye. And there it was: a mast a mile or two away. Wait, another one! Two masts ghosting on the tide towards the *Adventure*.

"Hell's bells," he yelled and ran to warn the two foolish crewmen in the stern, as well as the guests and small crew below. He yelled a warning aft and started down the ladder below but first looked up to confirm his observation before alarming men such as Blackbeard and Caesar.

He saw the orange flames and flashes before he heard the booming roar of four cannons firing their deadly iron balls. One whistled harmlessly through the rigging above. But to Smith's horror, the other three found their mark. The second ricocheted off the mast and decapitated one of the stern sailors. Three and four exploded on deck in a shower of large, deadly splinters, and small fires were erupting everywhere from the numerous lanterns.

The men below were already standing and Smith half screamed to Blackbeard and Caesar, "Two British sloops 'proachin' from the west, your lordships. Accurate gunners, one on deck kilt. Bow's on fire."

Smith stood back and watched Blackbeard process the information. Then he shed his newly acquired gentility and erupted in a torrent of orders to the crew within earshot. "Six to the cannons, four to fight fire, one to cut the cable and the rest of you heathens set sail!" Weapons were served out and Blackbeard was handed his leather bandolier that held three braces of pistols. As they started up the ladder, he quickly turned to Caesar with gleaming eyes and shouted, "Let's welcome our dinner guests with pirate lead and steel, shall we?"

Smith followed closely behind Caesar, who promptly stopped him. "No, boy, your place be here, below decks." Smith voiced his objection, but Caesar's eyes told him it was useless. He grabbed a large cutlass and stood at the bottom of the hatchway, noting the merchants were nowhere to be found.

As the pirates rushed on deck, they witnessed a perilous situation. Four more cannons had found their mark. Several dead pirates, broken rigging, fires, cannons upended and useless. It was a hellish scene. And now the *Adventure* shuddered abruptly and came to a halt on a sandbar because of the severed anchor cable and no steerageway with the rigging destroyed.

The closest boat, the Ranger, then slammed into the *Adventure* on the deep channel side and sailors and red-coated marines jumped on board and furious fighting commenced. The attack was led by a Lieutenant Robert Maynard, whose orders were to "eliminate the pirates," as Blackbeard was known to have slipped back into his pirate ways after receiving his pardon.

The pirates fought furiously but were outnumbered. Blackbeard had already struck down two sailors and a marine when three others engaged him with swords and bayoneted rifles. Each slashed and parried like cornered animals, but then Blackbeard suddenly crumpled to the ground, blood bubbling from his mouth.

"Filthy back-stabbin' coward. Show yourself … you bastard whelp which kilt Blackbeard."

Maynard stepped in front of him and looked into Blackbeard's dimming eyes. He slowly wiped the pirate's blood from his sword with a white silk handkerchief and said, "Lieutenant Robert Maynard, British Royal Navy."

Blackbeard started to speak, but Maynard plunged his sword though his heart and Blackbeard slumped to his death.

Caesar, who was fighting two sailors, saw this and howled, "Nooooo!" His friend and mentor was gone.

Maynard turned to the remaining combatants and shouted, "Drop your weapons now and in the King's name you will be spared." Seeing the man who was larger than life die in front of them took the fight out of the crew, and one by one they dropped their weapons and surrendered.

Caesar knew that with their guard dropped, he could kill a score of these British buggers, but then he too would eventually be killed. And that could not happen before he gave Smith a vital message for Kalos. So, he dropped his cutlass, short knife, pistols and belaying pin to the bloody deck. He and the prisoners were rounded up and forced below decks, guarded by the marines. There they were all met by a wild-eyed boy. With a large cutlass.

Smith eyed the bloody prisoners and saw Caesar was alive but did not see Blackbeard. "Where be Captain Blackbeard?" he demanded. No one answered, but the red-coated marines began to smirk. "Tell me where he be or I'll cut you bloody lobsters in half!"

Lieutenant Maynard, now descending the ladder, heard Smith and summed up the situation. "Lad, that seagoin' highwayman is dead and washing the deck with his yellow blood. And I suspect 'is ugly bearded head will be gracing a pike any minute."

True to his word, a now-hysterical Smith slashed wildly at the lieutenant's midsection, which Maynard effortlessly avoided. The officer then struck Smith's chin with the butt of his rifle and the boy was unconscious before his limp body bounced on the deck. Caesar was tense as a hawser under strain and swore an unintelligible oath. He knew he could rush the lieutenant and snap his neck like a chicken. But he had to stay alive. The smug and victorious officer ordered the marines to move the prisoners to the Ranger's brig and as an afterthought spent time peering through Blackbeard's logs and charts.

FOURTEEN

That night in the Ranger's brig, the pirates were all chained to a bulkhead, sitting on wet straw. Sleep was difficult as most pondered their fate, accompanied in the background by the sound of scurrying rats. They were headed to Williamsburg to be tried as pirates. It seemed that scurrilous Lieutenant Maynard's life-sparing statement was of short duration.

Before dawn, Caesar nudged Smith awake. "Morning, laddie. I sure am sorry for a gettin' you in this here predicament."18

Smith replied, "Please, your honor. This has been a grand journey. And I couldn't ask for a better shipmate."

Caesar stopped him and said, "The guards will be here soon. I have something very important to tell you, mate." And he began a litany of whispered instructions.

~~~

The pirates clinked and hobbled their way into a small wood-framed building that served as the region's courthouse. Smith's hands were bound with rough hemp as his wrists and hands were too small for iron restraints. As they shuffled along,
~~~

Caesar stealthily passed him a torn shirt and told the boy to wrap it around his head and jaw as best he could. He did so without question or raising the attention of the guards.

They were soon seated, and their numerouls crimes were recited slowly by a dandy in a white wig. At one point, Smith felt like his shipmates were rather proud of their litany of wrongdoings. Then one of the three judges said, "Your crimes have been cited. What say you to these charges?"

None dared speak until Caesar slowly stood up and, although weighted by shackles, extended himself to his full breadth and height. The courtroom's occupants edged back in their seats, glad the pirate was restrained.

"'Tis true, Your Honors. Many of those deeds were our doin'. Me and my shipmates—well, we weren't angels. We took from those that had to give. And most of them lived to see another sunrise, unless they crossed us. I never kilt a man who dinna try and kill me. But I ask one thing of Your Honors. Spare the boy. Show him the cat, put him in the brig, but don't stretch his scrawny neck. He was our blacksmith and a bad one he was. Weren't he, Ulysses?"

"That's right, guvnors. Never was worse. We was a-fixin' to keelhaul the bilge rat. Couldn't even put a good edge on a blade."

The other pirates, now understanding Caesar's unrehearsed plan, chimed in with their own invectives. "Turrble, turrble," they mumbled. "A one-armed monkey would make a better smith," one muttered.

Smith was stunned at hearing Caesar's dreadful entreaty and his shipmates' disparagement. He was part of the crew. They were his family. He couldn't let the captain do this. He started to rise and object when he felt a very strong four-fingered hand on his shoulder. Paddy had sensed Smith's mind and whispered, "Don't do it, laddie. Let the captain speak for you. Do it for him." Smith was full of conflicting emotions, but he calmed down reluctantly and watched Caesar carry on his oratory.

Caesar then directed his disdainful gaze to the far side of the makeshift courtroom. "Lieutenant Maynard," Caesar bellowed. The lieutenant's reverie about how his recent action would certainly result in a promotion was now disturbed. "When you smashed young Smith's jaw with your rifle butt, was he above decks fighting or was he a noncombatant situated below deck?"

The lieutenant, in a squirrely attempt to gather his wits, responded slowly and pompously. "Are you addressing me... you heathen?" Maynard quickly realized this pirate was no simpleton and he must answer carefully.

Caesar's initial volley on the lieutenant, however, struck its intended mark: the judges and others in the courtroom. English naval officers were held in high esteem and known throughout the world for their bravery, moral character and sense of honor. Beating on children greatly contradicted the archetype.

Caesar, sensing the tide of battle was shifting to his side, carried on. "Our Smith here, the young boy with the bandaged jaw. The one we carried unconscious to your pigsty of a brig. Did you knock him unconscious below decks, as witnessed by my crew? And by your Royal Marines? Or was he on deck furiously fighting for his life?" Not waiting for an answer, Caesar raised his voice, "We both know he was below decks, sir! Out of harm's way until you came along and shattered his jaw!"

Lieutenant Maynard's head was now spinning with confusion. Had this pirate outmaneuvered him? "Why, the boy had a foot-long cutlass," he retorted. "He swung it at me. Said he'd cut me half, he did!" At this, the pirate contingent burst out laughing.

The frustrated head judge's face turned beet red in high contrast to his gleaming white wig. "Order! Order! This is the King's court and I will have order!"

Caesar held up his hand and the pirates instantly stopped their mirth. Before the judge could rebuke them, Caesar said with a sly smile and a chuckle, "Well, I never served in His Majesty's Royal Navy…but on my ship, matey…we call a sword that size…a dairy knife!"

The entire courtroom erupted in laughter, including the judges. Now it was the lieutenant's turn to be red-faced. He began to sputter a reply, but Caesar melodramatically turned his back to him and addressed the judges. "Gents, you may think pirates are the scourge of the earth, but we are men of honor, and our word is our bond. And I swear to you to today on…on Neptune's eyes, the boy bain't no pirate. So, Your Honors, if you want to meet your maker with a clear conscience, I beseech you. Spare the boy."

Caesar sat down and there were various murmurs in the courtroom. The judges conferred for a few minutes, then reached an almost immediate consensus.

Death by hanging for all. Except the scrawny "Smith." Prison for the boy, but his life was spared. The hangings were to be carried out the next morning. The resigned pirate prisoners were led away and the boy was to be taken to a different part of the jail. As Caesar clinked and shuffled by, he locked eyes with Smith. His dark eyes were blazing and defiant, which gave Smith strength. Until his own eyes began to swell and tear. "Thank you, Captain. Goodbye," he said loudly. Then he was gone.

~~~

The sun woke Smith the next morning and he hobbled over to the small window in his cell. On his tiptoes he could see the town square where the hangings were to take place. It was crowded with people eager to see nine pirates swing from the
~~~

gallows. *Shallow, wicked people*, he thought. *Cowardly landlubbers who live meaningless lives. I pity them and I thank God for Caesar.*

The pirate captain stood stoically on the wooden platform, with closed eyes, inwardly knowing this freshly hewn deck was his last command. He stood straight and tough like the wood he carved. Caesar was always larger than life, but Smith was certain he saw him swell to an even greater size. As the hangman put a shroud over Caesar's head, the pirate roared, "Get that bleedin' thing offa me, ya filthy rottin' dough-faced son of a cow-poxed bitch!"

The hood was shakily removed and Caesar slowly surveyed the crowd. He spotted Smith in the window and smiled. Again, he roared, but this time to the crowd of merchants, busybodies and ghouls. "I am Ser'ada Ag Ilou by God. I am a Tuareg, son of Elfil Ag Khemidou. I was named Black Caesar by your stinkin' got-rottin' slavers and I will get my revenge on you in heaven or in hell! I am not afraid to meet my God. But by damn I wish I had the chance to help you gutless lubbers meet him too!"

Upon hearing his frightening tirade, several women in the crowd gasped, along with some faint-hearted men. Caesar found Smith again and winked as if to say, "I went out on my terms, my young friend, sounding like a twelve-pound cannon. Remember my instructions, matey." Then he let out a bellowing laugh that echoed through the square long after the hangman pulled his lethal lever. And the closest thing Smith had to a father was gone.

~~~

Kalos was gathering wood for his morning fire when his soul quivered. Once before Kalos had returned Caesar's lost soul to the living, but he could not help him now. His friend was gone. Kalos's eyes moistened as he crossed his arms and whispered to his sister, the wind. He told her what happened so the rest of world would also know. *I will miss him*, he thought. *Until I see him again. And now Smith and I must put Caesar's plan in to motion.*

~~~

PART THREE
ONE

Present Day
Miami, Florida

The sun felt good on my old bones. The deep heat combined with the boat's anchored motion lulled me into a daydream. I was transported to a similar day, a similar reef, four decades ago. Thinking about George's homemade scuba tank and him diving down and offering me a beer on the bottom made me smile. Damn, that was a great summer. So many lost summers since then. To this day I've never met anybody quite like George.

My reverie was broken by a watery commotion next to the boat. "Bill, Bill, I found something!" The surfacing diver was my adopted son, fifteen-year-old Ryan, who was lobstering below. This was the first day of Florida lobster season. The rest of the country goes berserk on the opening day of deer season. South Floridians go loco for lobster season.

I leaned over the gunwale and grabbed Ryan's tank, gear and lobster bag while he swam excitedly to the stern dive ladder. "Whatcha got?" I asked. But I knew the answer.

"Treasure!" he said excitedly. "Spanish

coins!"

How did I know? I secretly dropped two coins over the side while he was setting the anchor. I'd made sure they landed in sand so he would see them. They were a special gift from George to remind me that treasure was always around, but now it was Ryan's turn to appreciate them.

Ryan scurried up the stern ladder, dropped his fins and mask and held out his gloved hand holding two gold Spanish doubloons. He then asked suspiciously and slowly, "Hey … are these the coins George gave you?"

I smiled, knowing it would be a cold day in hell before I could put one over on this boy. In addition to being a techno genius, he was wise beyond his years. Sometimes I thought I was talking to an old man, a Viejo in Spanish.

He examined my face and said, "I knew it. I had a feeling." He smiled back at me. "But I thought he only gave you two coins." And he opened his other hand to reveal a third weathered doubloon.

~~~

What the hell!? Instantly it was 1967. Blue-headed turtles, funky yellow airplanes and George and I were hot on the trail of Caesar's gold. This was a topic I had buried deep in my subconscious. Ryan dropped the coins on the deck. Clink. Clank. A distant memory of a sound. What was it? Bingo!
~~~

The bulldozer running into the anchor ring.

Ryan was studying my face and eventually said, "Bill, are you having a stroke?"

"No, no," I stammered. "The third doubloon. I only dropped two. Where did you find it?"

"Over by two big brain corals."

"I need to see," I said shakily, so I threw on my scuba gear, James Bond style I might add, and hopped over the side. As soon as the bubbles cleared, I got the shivers in the bathtub-warm water. This was the same reef George and I caught our first lobster on! The brain corals had really grown, but this was it. I'd known we were in the general vicinity, but wow, what were the chances? After I calmed down, we scoured the reef together until we ran out of air, but no other coins or clues.

On the surface I said, "Let's head back, cook your lobsters, have some Key lime pie and ponder a bit. We both do better with full bellies." And with that we headed back home through the twisting and winding aquamarine channel known as Caesar Creek.

TWO

After a hasty boat and gear wash, we sat down over fried lobster and tart Key lime pie and discussed the discovery. Ryan started with, "Well, where do you think the doubloon came from?"

"Hmm … you and I dove the whole reef for any potential source and found none."

"Well, it had to come from somewhere."

"All I can think of is maybe it was just a single coin churned up by that tropical storm last month, or perhaps there is sunken treasure out here. But that area is no deeper than forty feet and heavily dived. Maybe it came from the HMS *Fowey*. It was discovered in 1975 not far from there."

We both sat mutely, contemplating our discovery. Ryan broke the silence and said, "Tell me more about George and Caesar." So, I transported myself back to that pivotal time in my life—1967. The Summer of Love. A time buried deep within me. I treasured all that George had taught me, but his view of the world was a tad myopic and couldn't pay for student loans, mortgage payments, etc. I still loved him and appreciated all he'd done for me, but frankly, George's wild tales and lifestyle simply didn't mesh with the course my life had taken.

After high school, I'd realized the Naval

Academy was not for me. Perhaps they'd realized it first. I thought I could sail their Luders yawls all day, but they had a thing about 4 a.m. shoeshines and strict military discipline. And I couldn't even begin to find a decent Key lime pie in Annapolis.

Ryan interrupted my daydreaming and said rather firmly, "Uh, Caesar. Legend. Focus, Bill. Please?" So, I told him everything I knew. I had only shared the whole story with Noelle before—no one else. Lord knows what happened to her. Last I heard she was in California. Telling Ryan everything now was rather cathartic, though. Details from a previously bottled-up portion of my mind began to emerge. Like unlocking a tomb or perhaps a secret treasure site. From the Grove to Cuba to the Caymans to Bimini to Elliott Key. Duppies, the Devil's Triangle, the anchor ring, a limestone turtle. I told Ryan everything. I even brought out one of the blue-headed turtles that he asked to study.

He soaked up the tale and all its cloudy details like a sponge. This was a kid who was solving Rubik's Cubes when he was five. I could see his wheels, or perhaps binary bits, spinning. When I was done, he simply said, "It's clear the limestone turtle is the key. We've got to get a look at it. If we do, I know we can solve this mystery."

Forty years ago, I would have been right there with him. Full steam ahead, damn the torpedoes! Toss me a greenie and drive! But I was a responsible adult. With a teenager. And frankly, the chances that there was a secret treasure and us finding it were as remote as living in a house built from a pier. I treasured the time I had with George. But I'd also read *Don Quixote* and it didn't end well for him. "This is my quest, to follow that star. No matter how hopeless. No matter how far." Key word being hopeless. I wasn't going to be disillusioned a second time.

"I know, I know," I said, "but that darn turtle is still with the Little family. After Dick's passing, due to a fortunate gun-cleaning accident, I thought his family would release the artifacts. Turns out they were as mean and nasty as he was." We finished our inaugural lobster season meal and retired with our individual pirate thoughts.

That night I lay awake, wondering if there was a connection between the Spanish gold coin and Caesar's legend. Or had it come from a shipwreck, fallen out of an unlucky seaman's pocket, washed out of a shoreline treasure horde? The reef was in the general vicinity of the supposed pirate camp. Should I restart an adventure that, seen through the looking glass of maturity, seemed hopelessly juvenile? Pirates forsooth!

Over the drone of the air conditioning, I could hear Ryan clicking away at his keyboard, the gateway to his maze of computers and beyond. I knew he'd be researching every bit of information he could get his hands on. He was probably writing an algorithm to compute storm wind and tide patterns and the resultant effects on a gold coin.

Ryan's computer skills were scary. He was something special and born with a gift. In fact, it's the reason we met in the first case. Ryan had been in foster care since he was five. His computer aptitude was off the charts, but he often used his skills for less than *upright* means. After the umpteenth unauthorized money transfer, grade switch and foray into the occasional defense contractor database, Ryan landed on my doorstep at the behest of a good friend of mine. He said Ryan's next incursion into the digital dark side would land him in juvie, which he was ill equipped to deal with.

Having just retired from the accounting profession (I know, don't tell George), I accepted the challenge and arrangement. In my inexpert opinion, I thought he simply had too much energy and time, i.e., the old "idle hands are the devil's playground" saying.

So, after several unreported missteps involving agents in black suits from initialed agencies dropping by to offer (and receive) advice, I embarked on a plan to expose Ryan to an outdoor life. I didn't know much about the digital world, but the saltwater world was where I used to feel at home. Sailing, fishing and diving can have a magical effect on you. It's real. Makes you self-reliant. It's not a made-up world of dungeons and dragons. It provides success if you work hard and teaches you a hard lesson when you don't.

So, I began to immerse us both into a world I

had left behind. This new voyage began with the purchase of a sweet center console fishing boat with twin 250s and the latest in nautical electronics.

When he first moved in, Ryan would stay up all night, drink Mountain Dew and do things on the computer I didn't understand. But after fighting a few fifty-pound dorado and tuna, spearfishing the inquisitive hog snapper or capturing bagsful of lobster, he was hooked, so to speak. So now he maintained a healthy balance of an outdoor and indoor life, because face it, his computer talent was a gift and shouldn't be wasted.

And in my perhaps quixotic task to help Ryan, I too began to feel more alive. A pilot light was lit in my repressed inner soul and was starting to burn a little brighter every day.

The next morning over black coffee, banana pancakes and more fried lobster, Ryan suggested that we drive by George's house, Shangri-La, for motivation. I was nostalgic for George and his lair, the starting point for so many of our adventures. I agreed and thought maybe, just possibly, we could divine some inspiration.

THREE

It was gone. Shangri-La was Shangri-Nah. Replaced with a two-story monolithic McMansion. I couldn't even see if his trees or even the crazy turtle pond remained. The wellspring of so many exploits gone. I shouldn't have been surprised. It was happening all over Miami. Old houses on big lots, torn down and replaced with large and hideous odes to owners' egos. Soulless architecture. Soulless people.

Didn't they realize what it took to build that house? George dragged a goddamn pier for miles to build it. I wish I was there when they tore it down. I pictured a wrecking ball hitting the house, then ricocheting backward, spinning wildly around the crane like a one-sided tether ball game. And the cigar-chomping operator gruffly exclaims, "What the hell is this house made of?"

"Pier!" I say smugly.

Ryan disregarded my disappointment and asked, "Is he buried in Miami?"

"Yep," I replied curtly.

"Well, heck, while we're out let's go visit and pay our respects. I'd like to meet him. Maybe there's inspiration there?"

"No," I said. The sight of Shangri-La missing was just too depressing. Old ghost stories, near death experiences. So much safer to leave them interred where they couldn't haunt me.

But Ryan pressed on. Determined. Reminded me of … me. Then he got me. "You owe it to George, goddamn it."

We headed out to the cemetery on the west side of Miami, parked and walked slowly up to his plot. There on his headstone: George Henderson-Stein. Still makes me laugh. Ryan and I stood there respectfully, lost in thought.

I finally spoke. "George, it's me, Bill … I mean Billy. I'm sorry I've stayed away for so long. I brought my son Ryan."

"Hi, George, it's nice to meet you."

I knew we sounded like two crazy people, but there were things I had to say. "George, you wouldn't approve of the life I chose. It was lucrative but colorless. But I'm back. With Ryan's help. I just took a little detour, okay? I just bought a boat. You wouldn't believe it, twin engines. Same concept as Mr. Porter's, but on steroids. Uh, steroids are things that make you … never mind. Anyhow. Big news. Remember that reef we dove on with the fire extinguisher scuba tank? Well, Ryan found a doubloon there! Can you believe it? We looked all over the reef and didn't find anything else, but I'll bet we're close. Do you think Caesar hid the treasure in the patch reefs? Makes sense as Elliott Key is so small and a treasure-filled hole would have been discovered by now."

I continued. "Oh, that piece of dog shit Little

died. I know it's probably wrong, but his grave smells like a fire hydrant in a dog park. Don't ask me how, but I kept my promise. Rest assured. Okay, bad choice of words. Trust me, George, we will see that old turtle and find the clue it's hiding. Ryan here is smart as they come with computers and the internet." Ryan looked at me puzzled—as if George knew what the internet was. "Well, listen, George, the landscaping here is fine, but I think the place could use a few flowers. The duppies will appreciate it too. There's a vendor down the street. We'll be right back." I almost said, "don't go anywhere."

Ryan and I walked to a nearby flower stand, and upon our return, our jaws dropped. Right on top of the gravestone was a blue-headed turtle. Some fifty years after I'd viewed the last one. *Holy shit*, I thought.

"Holy shit," Ryan said out loud. "This is way cool." I had a clear view in all directions but didn't see a soul. Once again, we were being directed by an unknown source to solve a centuries-old mystery.

We stayed a few more moments, and as Ryan looked intently at the wooden turtle, I spoke inwardly to George, and whoever else might be listening, imploring them with all my soul to please help me solve this mystery.

FOUR

Ryan and I had a morning ritual. We would take turns making Cuban coffee and the other would warm up pastelitos con guayaba. Sometimes con queso. It was always a contest to see who could produce the most espumita, the sweet foam on top of the sugary espresso. Both the coffee and the pastry are absolutely sinful and provide an eye-opening kick of caffeine and sugar in the morning. It's safe to say that Miami runs on cafecitos and its big brother, the colada. We would then enjoy these delicacies while reading the morning news. Me on traditional newsprint and he on his tablet gizmo. It was a nice way to start the day, discussing current events.

On this day I mentioned that the Dolphins were in training camp and I began to regale Ryan with the success of the 1972 team, which didn't elicit much interest from him. Another article caught my eye. "Hey, did you see the Coast Guard lost a new million-dollar drone?" I asked.

Ryan coughed and said, "No, what happened?"

"Seems they were testing it for search and rescue missions and it flat out disappeared. I swear. Typical government waste. And you and I pay for such ineptitude."

Ryan then said, "I was thinking. Since we can't get our hands on the limestone turtle, why don't we visit someone who carved and shaped things out of limestone?"

"Who's that?" I asked.

"Karl Kahn."

"Who's that?"

"Uh, only the man who built Coral Castle!"

"Oh, c'mon. He's been dead for fifty years and was half crazy."

"Crazy like a fox. C'mon, Bill, let's take a drive." So, we fired up Foxy Lady, my Mini Moke, and headed south on US-1.

Coral Castle is a quirky Miami tourist attraction. Constructed over a period of thirty years, it was built entirely from limestone with some slabs weighing over ten thousand pounds. It contains numerous fantasy architectural elements, including whimsical furniture and astrological symbols. But to this day no one knows how one small man could accomplish so much without modern machinery and equipment. One thing that is known is that he used sharpened car leaf springs to chisel and free the big blocks from the ground. You can even see their marks today.

As we took the Castle tour, it really was astounding what he was able to accomplish. We were both interested in some animal figurines carved out of limestone. I asked the guide how he was able to be so intricate. The guide replied, "Look closely. You'll see seams where he joined limbs and appendages in places the limestone was impossible to carve."

"What was the seam filler made of?"

"Well, we don't rightly know, but one of the working theories is he used a Tequesta pottery trick by mixing plant material in a limestone slurry so when it dried it resembled the pattern of the rock, rendering the seam almost invisible." A small light bulb started to glow in my head and I could tell Ryan had a more advanced LED going.

At the end of the tour we viewed his tool shed, which held a variety of odd implements, including some old photographs of Karl back in the day. One caught my eye. It showed Karl working, but in the background there stood an enormous three-story-high tripod. It resembled a modern-day drilling rig or derrick. My mind went back to the day in the Grove library where I'd read about the Tuareg. Was this how they dug wells? Was this how the anchor hole was dug? Seemed like overkill. Could larger holes be dug? In the ocean? My mind was racing, and I secretly thanked George for starting this mission and to whomever or whatever had placed the blue-headed turtles to keep us motivated.

As we exited the attraction, I said, "Hey, let's head over to the Dunkers for a fresh strawberry shake. If we're lucky, maybe we can pick up a bag of Key limes too."

FIVE

Days went by and I introduced Ryan into the rituals of a South Florida boyhood. I showed him how to mow neighbors' yards for a bit more than George paid me and he in turn wrote a program indicating the optimal mowing pattern based on a digital property survey and mower blade dimensions. "Why sweat more than you must?" he reasoned.

But it was the mango business where he really excelled. We built a mango stand together out of scrap wood and hoped he'd sell enough of our mangoes to buy some new fishing equipment. A week or two went by and I noticed Ryan wasn't working the stand much. I asked him why and he said it was under control. He saw my nervous face, smiled and said, "Let's go check it out."

We walked the two blocks to a vacant lot where he'd set up shop. Along the way I noticed every mango tree was bare. On arrival, cars were backed up five deep and high school cheerleaders were selling for him. It was quite a sight, but I didn't know whether to be proud or upset.

On the way home, I grilled him on where he'd gotten all those mangoes as our two trees wouldn't last a day at that pace. After much hemming and hawing, I learned he'd subcontracted the supply side of the business to a nefarious gang of ten-year olds who disappeared after dinner each night with empty five-gallon buckets. They magically appeared full on the side of our house several hours later—much to the chagrin of the citizens of Pinecrest and its reluctantly dieting squirrel population. Early the next day, Ryan would size and categorize them, pay the ringleader, Cole, and then Phil from Native Son Landscaping would transport them to the stand with his trailer. The only real problem, for me, was that Phil's old truck leaked red brake fluid on my otherwise pristine concrete driveway.

Phil was an old friend who was reliable, but a tad quirky. He was also extremely hard of hearing, which I attributed to years of leaf blowers and Black Sabbath tribute bands. So, communications had to be face-to-face and often involved a system of hand gestures worthy of an Italian traffic cop.

"What about the cheerleaders?" I asked.

"Bill," he said somewhat sardonically, "the premium I can tack onto the market price more than offsets my increased payroll. Aren't you familiar with the elasticity of demand?"

I switched topics and said, "Well, where did you find your customers?"

He replied slowly. "Ya know the Fairchild Garden Mango Festival?"

"Of course. It's fantastic! Every kind of mango in the world, practically."

"Yeah, well, their email list is not very well

protected."

"What?! We had an agreement."

"Hey, I did them a service. I even fixed their sieve of a firewall and sent their IT guy an email with some recommendations." Jeesh. It was hard to stay mad for long, and he did donate a portion of his proceeds back to the Garden.

SIX

Several frustrating weeks went by and we both spent time researching what we could on Black Caesar. I had even started going through my mother's old DAR papers, trying to find Caesar's trial records. A daunting task. Ryan assisted by scanning everything to what he called a drop box. Sounded like a Cold War spy craft thing to me.

One morning, during our ritual reading of the Miami *Tribune*, we both said, "Whoa!" Ryan was faster. "Bill! The Little family is in the paper."

And I said, "They're donating all their Native American artifacts to the Historical Museum and the Seminole Tribe." There was even a picture of several pieces, including the limestone turtle. This was our chance!

Turns out the entire family had a gambling problem, as evidenced by their running up a monstrous tab at the local Seminole gaming facility. When the tribal leaders became aware of the debt, they suggested a fair trade. All the family's ill-gotten artifacts were to be donated to the Miami Historical Museum and their own Ah-Tah-Thi-Ki museum. Either this or the offenders were alligator bait. I made that up. Alligators don't eat rotten meat.

The article said the artifacts, including the

now-named Tequesta Turtle, would be on special display in a month. "So, let's go get it," Ryan said.

"Hold on," I said. "I'm not going to steal anything. People go to jail for that. I'm not risking that for me or you."

We both sat silent for a bit until Ryan said, "What if we just borr…ow…ed it? For a bit? Either there are clues or there aren't. And if we can't figure it out, then we don't deserve to solve the mystery anyhow."

"Hmm, you have a point." So that morning over black coffee, the quest to solve a three-century-old legend was reborn.

My part required procuring a large panel van, an air -conditioning compressor box, a wooden pallet, a hydraulic dolly, coveralls and surgical tools. I planned on renting the van, but the AC stuff involved a small favor. I called an old client, Rick at Grovey Air, and made my appeal. Rick thought about it, and after he hesitated too long, I reminded him that the statute of limitations had not run out on a certain Guatemalan adventure we'd once taken.

"When and where do you want the stuff?" Rick responded half-heartedly.

While I was working logistics, Ryan was working the technology angle. The first big-ticket item we needed was access to a large 3-D printer. I wasn't even sure what the hell that was, but thankfully Ryan was taking several advanced computer courses at the University of Miami. He said his professor, Dr. Singer, was always up for a fun project and he'd probably earn extra credit. He was also working on some spectral photo image thingy. At some point I had to let him run with his side of the plan.

I was feeling good. Sometimes you need an element of danger in your life to be truly alive. And I needed to feel alive.

SEVEN

The plan came to fruition over a three-week period, but then we started making ourselves crazy with anticipation, so I suggested running over to Bimini for a few days. Our plan was to head over on Friday and return Sunday, which would still leave us a few days before the grand opening of the exhibit.

With the boat loaded, we took off across the bay, ran through Stiltsville and headed to Bimini. Land of Hemingway, rum-running and adventure. Sure brought back lots of memories. I started to instruct Ryan on how to steer ninety-five degrees by compass, and he reminded me that the GPS plotter and autopilot were already dialed in. "Well, then, don't hit anything," I said and took a nap.

Ryan woke me when were 6.337 nautical miles off South Bimini. I started to instruct him how the range markers worked and he in turn relished showing me how the digital chart depicted real channel markers now.

"Can I at least pilot us in to the Sands of Bimini resort?"

"Sure Bill, but I already programmed it." Jeesh, what was the nautical world coming to?

We were staying on South Bimini as I couldn't find a room on North Bimini. Big things had come to this island so steeped in legendary saltwater lore. Primarily gambling and a huge development north of Alice Town.

After clearing customs and checking into our room, I suggested running up to north Bimini and checking out the Compleat Angler. It would be fun to show Ryan all the old fishing pics, even the one with a juvenile George.

We tied up at the Bluewater docks and headed for the Angler. But it wasn't there. Only the stone chimney. We learned the wood-framed building had sadly burned down, taking with it precious photographic memories and, more precious, the life of its proprietor. I was getting maudlin, so we wandered over to the Red Lion for a greenie, some cracked conch and fried hog snapper. We meandered up and down the Queen's Highway, which is oxymoronic, for a bit, then headed back to the Sands.

The next morning, we headed north to dive the Steps to Atlantis. It was easy to find now. No shore bearings needed like George used. Thank goodness they were still there. Pretty, but there were plenty of other boats there. And it turns out there was a logical reason for the Steps. Geologists had confirmed it was just a natural stone formation. No more legendary road descending to the depths of an antediluvian underwater city of wonder.

Fishing changed too. In the '60s you found a reef, dropped a baited hook over the side and pulled up a grouper or snapper. Today, technology and machinery had taken over. People were now using electric reels to fish seven hundred feet down, producing, admittedly, delicious yellow-eyed snapper and blackbelly rose fish. Once, wahoo were considered a rarity, and now they were targeted by trolling at twenty knots with weights and wire line and oversized reels. The fish didn't have a chance. Maybe I didn't either.

After a quick bite of conch salad on crackers with a drop of hot sauce, we headed south to check out the SS *Sapona*. Was she there? As we turned the corner on South Bimini, there she was. A relic from a time gone by. A little worse for wear. But she'd endured where many hadn't. Was there a lesson here? Several boats were diving around her, and frankly it was nice she was still serving a purpose. Something one ponders when one reaches my age.

We headed slowly back to the Sands of Bimini and Ryan observed I was a little down. "C'mon, Bill, you know the only thing constant is change. Let's look forward to examining the turtle."

"Yeah, you're right," I said and tried to pick up my mood. Once back onshore, I realized the locals were happy with the increased prosperity the casinos and new developments brought to the island. But to me, Bimini was losing its charm fast. Just like Key West when the cruise ships first sailed in. David Allan Coe sang Cayo Hueso's obituary best with the satirical "Jimmy Buffet doesn't live in Key West anymore."

The return trip started off pleasantly. But halfway across, I noticed a dark, fast-moving squall approaching from the southwest. Low, dark scudding clouds. Ominous. A real Devil's Triangle storm. It was going to be bad. Real bad. I told Ryan to put his foul weather gear on, stow anything loose and lock all the hatches. I braced mentally and physically to get us through the upcoming maelstrom. Then Ryan turned on our digital radar and pointed out that the squall, although violent, was not particularly big and we'd be through the worst of it in thirty minutes. I would never consciously seek out trouble, but I had been looking forward to a bit of danger.

EIGHT

It was now three days before the exhibit opening. The event was getting a lot of press, and many local politicians, luminaries and up-and-coming Ponzi schemers would be in attendance. I don't mind telling you, I was nervous as hell, but I wasn't going to let George down.

The 3-D printer had finished its task. It had taken almost a week and Ryan said he would need help moving the output. He was also looking forward to introducing me to Dr. Singer. So, we headed over to the lushly landscaped campus, parked near the Rathskeller and walked to the Industrial Engineering Building.

Several corridors and doors later, there she was. A perfect replica of the Tequesta Turtle. I was staring at it almost emotionally. She was beautiful and maybe the key to unlocking a mystery that had intrigued and haunted me for decades.

After a few gawking moments, a small cough alerted me that Ryan was standing with Dr. Singer. We exchanged pleasantries and he told me how extraordinary Ryan was and what fun they'd had on this project. They lost me when their small talk turned to tangential spherical geometry, but my general focus returned when they discussed having enlisted the services of another professor to assist.

A Dr. DeSolle, an expert in oceanic animals. Ryan had never mentioned anyone else, and frankly, I was a bit concerned as the fewer people involved, the better.

While we continued the small talk, the other professor appeared. Her jaw dropped, which I assumed mimicked mine. It was Noelle. Professor Noelle DeSolle, marine biologist.

I was stunned. And she was still beautiful. A mature woman, but also the fifteen-year-old girl of my teenage dreams. After our mutual initial surprise, she gave me a warm hug, which I awkwardly returned.

We made small talk for a bit until I mentioned we were on a timetable. Ryan and I gingerly picked up the turtle. It was light but bulky and required two people to carry it. As we crab-walked away, Noelle pushed her business card into my shirt pocket and whispered, "Hey, landscaper, don't be a stranger."

In the car Ryan asked, "You know Professor DeSolle?"

"She was my first love," I said. "And I don't want to talk about it, okay?"

"Okay, that's fair." Then he proceeded to say, "If you ever want to talk, I'm a really good listener. Relationships old or new can be very taxing emotionally. It's good for the soul to let your feelings out. Cathartic even. I'm here for you in any event." *There he goes, an old man in a boy's body.*

That night I sat on the edge of my bed and rolled Noelle's card over and over again in my embarrassingly moist hands. Noelle DelSolle, marine biologist. Strange how someone who'd occupied so much of my youthful mind eventually became relegated to a place adjacent to a dusty legend. Was I subconsciously seeking both now? We were a thing through junior year until I'd seen her in the backseat of a cherry-red Camaro. I'd never talked to her again and then her father was transferred soon after. That was it, never heard about her again. I'd searched for her on Facebook once but found nothing. I'd assumed she was gone forever.

So, in the spirit of what the fuck, which was a common theme lately, I called. "Hello, Noelle? It's Bill … Billy. Too late to call?"

"No—no, I'm glad you did. How are you?"

"Good. Crazy, but good. So how does one start a conversation after forty years."

She laughingly replied, "Baby steps. Tell me about Ryan. Dr. Singer told me he's beyond gifted and wise for his years."

As any proud parent would, I launched into a Ryan dialogue and we then merged into a familiar territory of shared interests and emotions. She had been married to a Mr. DeSolle from France. He was an international cardboard salesman who, unlike Jim Morrison, eventually failed to light her fire. We talked for at least an hour and ended it with a dinner date the following night in Coral Gables.

I wanted to suggest a romantic French restaurant with a good Shadow Bree Ond. But it was too soon. That was a magical night long ago and to rush or even try to recreate anything similar would be like hitting an off-key note in a beautifully intricate melody.

Italian cuisine seemed safe and we agreed to meet at Café Pomona at seven. With the scent of baked garlic hanging in the air, I started the conversation off by asking how she'd gotten into the marine sciences.

She replied, "It's not obvious? You and George inspired me! You both loved the ocean so much and had so many seaborne escapades, I wanted a profession where I could find that kind of passion and sense of adventure."

Who knew George and I were that inspirational? The rest of the night, we filled each other in on the past forty years. The '70s and '80s over antipasto and the '90s and 2000s over a shared Caesar salad. The 2010s through the present were over sinful manicotti and lasagna. She was still beautiful, but no longer innocent. Not that she had seen evil, but like me, she had seen the good, the bad and the ugly of life. I think we mutually yearned for those innocent days in the Grove where our lives had intertwined with a legend.

As dinner was winding down, I absentmindedly said I'd kill for a good piece of Key lime pie. Noelle's eyes brightened as she replied, "I make a killer Key lime pie! Almost as good as George's."

There it was. We had stayed away from that time period. Too sensitive. *You always remember vividly the girl you share your first piratical quest with*, I thought, smiling inwardly. But now it was out there.

"That's some big talk."

"Well, come over and tell me I'm wrong to my face," she said with a smile.

"You're on," I challenged.

She didn't give me the address but simply winked and said, "Follow me."

I shadowed her through the shaded, ornate streets of Coral Gables to the even more canopied but less ornate streets of Coconut Grove. We weaved our way into George's old neighborhood, and I wondered if Gwendolyn the alligator still lived nearby. I was lost in thought when her turn signal lit up, a gate opened and she turned into the McMansion that was previously Shangri-La.

You've got to be fuckin' kidding me! Then I heard a fifteen-year-old Billy say, "Be diplomatic, okay? We may only have one shot at this. No insults. The past is the past. Let bygones be bygones. Love thy neighbor. Peace, love and happiness. Just like the hippies, okay? Swallow your pride."

I followed her and got out my car with my prior self's sage advice ringing in my ear. "Are you fucking kidding me?" I yelled. "How the fuck could you do this? To me? To George?"

She stared at me incredulously. "I thought you'd be surprised and happy."

She went on to explain, but I heard nothing. One more dagger in my heart. After a lifetime of daggers, your heart grows callous. An evolutionary mechanism kicks in, the pain is diminished and the organism moves into self-preservation mode. While I retreated emotionally, she advanced and took my hand. I was in a rage but too confused to do anything about it. She guided me to the side of the property.

There was our table, under the big tree with twinkly lights. With two roses in a small clear vase. I looked at her and a multitude of emotions must have crossed my face. Wonder, awe, admiration, curiosity. I finally started to listen.

"You haven't heard a single word I've said, have you?" she asked.

"I'm sorry. I'm so confused. What's this all about?"

"Well, first, I didn't knock George's house down. But after you sold it, you had to know someone would eventually. I simply bought the house that was here. I wanted to preserve the spot where I spent one of the greatest nights of my life."

I mumbled a thank-you, and after emotions died down, we silently ate her Key lime pie. It was delicious. Tart, blending to sweet, then tart again. A good Key lime pie should make your lips pucker. Like two teenagers sharing their first kiss in a jasmine-scented garden on a magical night. More

Key lime juice than a typical recipe calls for. That's what makes a great Key lime pie and separates the tourist version from the local. There was something different in the crust, though. I made a mental note to ask later.

After some small talk, she eventually said, "Now what's with the turtle, really?"

I hesitated in my reply. I wasn't sure whether to tell her or not. After all, she'd been absent from my life for decades. But the last few weeks seemed like the heavens were aligning in a way I could have never imagined. Here I was in George's garden. Reliving a moment that was virtually uncreatable. But here we were. So, I revealed everything to her, just like I had done some forty years ago.

She took it all in as Ryan did. Except she had a head start. After a brief contemplation she said, "I want in."

I said, "That's not possible. You have a respectable job with the university, and this could destroy your career."

Out of nowhere, and in a funny feminine pirate brogue, she announced. "But I can help you matey!" To which we both roared with laughter. She went on to say, "Look, I'm a marine biologist and frankly, you could use my skills and resources." There were only a few things I'd learned with certainty in my life, and two of them were never turn down a helping hand and never,

ever stand in the way of a smart, determined woman on a mission.

NINE

In the days leading up to the opening, Noelle offered assistance where she could, but I drew the line on her being present at the "heist." She had more to lose than we did.

Finally, the day had arrived. We were going to get a look at the Tequesta Turtle up close. Either that or a night in the pokey, the slammer, the crowbar hotel. Our plan was to arrive downtown at noon on the day of the official evening opening of the new Artifacts Exhibit. We figured there would be just the right amount of commotion to cover our investigation.

At the house we put on overalls that said Legend Air, matching the temporary sign on the van. Ryan, noting both, said, "Nice touch, Bill."

We drove downtown and parked in a loading zone. At 11:50 a.m., Ryan broke out his laptop and promptly hacked into the museum's building management systems. He overrode the thermostats and within minutes the building began to get very warm. After all, it was a typical hot, steamy Florida day and nothing but air blown over freezing cold pipes containing condensing freon could stop this muggy heat.

I walked up to the already sweat-stained receptionist and said, "I'm here to save the day."

"Oh, thank goodness. We have a big event planned tonight. Thank you. Thank you."

I went back to the van, and we unloaded the large compressor box with all the materials we needed inside. Soon we were pushing the box on the hydraulic dolly down the museum's hallways on the way to the Tequesta Turtle.

We slowed to survey the area. "Huh, you feel that?" I said to Ryan. The AC was back on!

Ryan opened his laptop and was furiously clicking away when the receptionist rushed up. "Hey, fellas. Our security guard found an emergency override on the AC controls and it appears to be working now. Can you come back after the exhibit opening? We really don't need any more turmoil."

Ryan and I looked blankly at each other and I muttered a weak "okay." We turned the dolly around and reversed course back to the van.

I wanted to cuss like a marooned sailor, but this situation called for a cool head. After the exhibit opening, the turtle would be moved behind armored glass and we'd never get a shot like this again. We sat silently and morosely in the front seat. I ran through all the fantastic events that had gotten us to this point. We were so close and it was all being ripped away.

"I may … have a solution," Ryan mumbled under his breath. I looked at him hopefully. Then hesitantly. Then nervously.

"What do you have in mind?" I asked

apprehensively.

"It'll be easier to show you." And he motioned me to the back of the van. There was another box, hidden under a moving pad, that I hadn't noticed. Ryan pulled off the cover and in the dim light it appeared to be some kind of flying contraption. He flipped on the van's dome light, which revealed a very expensive-looking drone. Real high-tech stuff. It was painted orange and white. With black stenciled letters. USCG.

"That's the Coast Guard drone the newspaper was talking about. Are you crazy? We're breaking major laws here!" I exclaimed.

"Relax, Bill. I'm just borrowing it."

I was speechless. "Why is that little red light blinking?"

"Oh, that's like an EPIRB. It's telling CAMSLANT in Virginia where the drone is located."

"Great," I said. I could hear the wailing police sirens, the pounding of the judge's gavel and the clank of the jail door closing.

"Relax, Bill," Ryan said. "I overrode the GPS chip with a lat-lon algorithm. It's telling the operator the drone is in Riverside, Iowa, the future birthplace of Captain James T. Kirk."

That's fantastic, I thought to myself, *I feel so much better.*

"Before I call Roy Black, explain to me again why you took it."

"Well, I had heard about the project, so I

reviewed the contactor's design specs and saw several major flaws. One of which was that the device was subject to hijacking, as evidenced by the fact that I have it." I felt he wasn't telling me the whole story, but I let him continue. "Well, this was such an important project, I just had to borrow the drone and fix it. Ya know, I'm pretty good at this kind of stuff."

"So why is it here? Today?"

"Bill, no plan is ever perfect," he said seriously, "and I thought we might need a backup today."

By now my brain was numb and I said, "So what's your plan, Houdini?"

"Well, that manual override the guard triggered has me locked out. I'm sure I could write a bypass, but that will take some time. Here's what I think we should do."

After listening for a minute, I gave him the go-ahead and wondered if my jail cell would have a western exposure. You know, for the romantic sunsets over the barbed-wire-topped wall.

We carried the drone box to the adjacent alley and Ryan skillfully launched it skyward. Soon it was hovering over the museum roof, its search-and-rescue target now being the museum's cooling tower. The building used a chilled water system to cool the interior space. The compressors generating the cooling also generated heat, so they needed to be cooled by a water loop, much like a car radiator. The cooling tower, in effect, cooled the compressors. If the cooling tower shut down, then the compressors automatically shut down to protect themselves and voilà—a hot building once again.

Ryan deftly maneuvered the drone over the cooling tower and delicately placed a wooden dowel right into one of its blades, stopping it. We jogged back to the van and the receptionist was already there. "Thank goodness I caught you. It's getting hot again! Can you do something?"

"I don't know. We just received a call over at the Science Museum …"

"Please, I'm begging."

"Okay, okay. I think we can help."

Once again Ryan and I pushed and pulled the dolly into the building.

We were next to the turtle now and Ryan hit a few strokes on his tablet. Darkness. Building management systems were wonderful if you wanted to borrow a three-hundred-year-old turtle. With the lights out, I opened the box with the duplicate turtle inside. It wasn't perfect, but it was light and would do the trick. We exchanged the original with the phony version with a few grunts, and in less than a minute we had made the switch and the lights were back on.

We arrived at the freight elevator and pushed the dolly in, closed the door and hit the off switch. Ryan pulled off the box and there she was. I had waited a lifetime to see her up close. She was beautiful, almost modernistic in style. The turtle had obviously been cleaned up, probably by Little, and no obvious evidence of a blue head.

Ryan handed me a pair of goggles, doused the elevator light and pulled out a crazy-looking square-headed flashlight hooked up to a digital thingy-scope. He shined the light on the head of the turtle and began turning knobs on his contraption. After a minute or two, several small patches on the turtle's head began to glow.

"That's it!" Ryan announced excitedly. "That's it. The limestone is porous, so it was impossible to clean every trace of ancient dye. The turtle's head was once painted blue, or more accurately, indigo. Without a doubt this was a blue-headed or rather a blue-turbaned turtle at one time."

I can't lie. I almost peed myself, but Ryan kept up his scientific investigation. With the elevator light back on he brought out the surgeon's tools and magnifying glasses and proceeded to inspect and gently pick all over the turtle's surface. When he got near the tail he said, "Gotcha!"

What? Got what? I was literally hopping up and down when he handed me the surgeon's loupe magnifiers.

"Look here. See the seam? Just like at Coral Castle." The turtle wasn't all one piece; the tail was separate.

By now we were sweating profusely from the lack of AC and the nerves we were experiencing. We were running out of time, so I grabbed the tail and wiggled it. Nothing. Then I pulled. Then I tried again with all my might. Nothing. I flashed back to all the clues George and I had uncovered—all pointing to this turtle—and I gave one more heave and ended up on the elevator floor holding a limestone turtle tail.

The missing tail revealed a long, hollow cavity within the turtle. Ryan shined his light in and then slowly removed a long, dark cylindrical piece of wood covered in markings. As we withdrew the brown rod from the cavity, we wanted to laugh like silly, juvenile schoolboys on the playground. But we heard more commotion outside, so we had no time to study or even contemplate what we just discovered. I pushed the tail back on and covered the turtle with the box while Ryan used the drone to remove the wooden dowel from the cooling tower. We then returned to the turtle's new home, where we reversed our steps by turning off the lights and pulled the turtle switcheroo without a hitch.

As we exited the building, it looked like we'd replaced a compressor in record time and had to turn the power off briefly. All without suspicion. When people are hot in Miami, logic goes out the window. Just get the damn air conditioning on, man. At the exit, the receptionist thanked us for making it cool again but did a double take when Ryan said in a gruff voice, "You're welcome, ma'am."

We loaded everything up at the van and Ryan

retrieved the drone. I was about to pull onto the street when a police officer knocked on my window. The officer said, "Good afternoon. We've had a lot of thefts in the area, and I just called Legend Air. Did you know you have no phone number? Odd, huh? Mind if I see what's in the back?"

My initial thought was *Sure, there's nothing there but a plastic turtle, a light gizmo and an old stick. Oh, and a million-dollar drone on "loan" from the Coast Guard.* So, I started to stammer a reply when a car pulled up suddenly behind the officer.

The occupant yelled excitedly, "Officer, Officer, two men just robbed the First Bank of Miami. Dark blue hoodies. Headed east on Flagler. Hurry, they're getting away!" He immediately bolted in the bank's direction and I made eye contact with the Good Samaritan citizen. Noelle to the rescue. She simply mouthed the words "You're welcome" and sped away.

During the drive I felt oddly alive. Like I was fifteen. No aches and pains. Just a wonderful feeling of vitality no matter how this turned out. If George could see us now. I think he'd celebrate at Marcella's with a big pizza, but of course she sadly closed her doors years ago.

TEN

Noelle met us at the house and we picked at a Key lime pie and stared at the wooden rod on the dining room table. It was covered in what looked like scrimshaw or hieroglyphics. The rod was about two feet long and the wood was unusual. Or was it? I grabbed the most recent blue-headed turtle and held it against the wooden rod. Identical in grain and color. George had called it lignum vitae and it was rare and durable.

Ryan took pictures of the symbols and sent them to the far corners of the web for deciphering. While he was doing his thing, I brewed up some Cuban coffee, which Noelle and I sipped at my tiled dining table. She was doodling some of the images from the rod, but the tile grout lines were ruining her artful doodles. She brought up a conversation we'd started long ago but never finished.

"So, what do you think Caesar was like?" she asked. Good question.

I paused and said, "He was probably authoritative, smart, even articulate. I think he was a victim of circumstance. Something forced him into piracy. And I don't believe he was bloodthirsty either. I believe it was a business for him."

We discussed Caesar for a while before Ryan

emerged from his room. He said, "Bill, I'm not getting anywhere. These characters don't seem to exist anywhere in the world. Current or historical."

Noelle listened to Ryan's frustration and continued her doodling when she straightened up suddenly in her chair. Cuban coffee can have that effect, but then she said, "Hand me the rod, please." She then placed her doodling paper on the rod, pressed down on a few characters, then lightly drew on the resulting imprint. The image was now reversed.

I saw where she was going with this, so I took the rod and rolled it firmly across a larger piece of paper, creating indentations. Then I took a pencil and lightly shaded over the imprints to reveal the characters in reverse. It was like an old typeset printing machine. "Wow! Whoever carved this did so in a mirror image, which was no easy mental or physical task."

Now Ryan was able to use his skills once again and reversed all the characters. He quickly determined that the language was Tuareg, confirming my long-ago suspicion, and consisted primarily of numbers. Ryan stared at the seemingly random figures and asked, "Could they be latitude and longitude?"

"No," Noelle interjected, "I don't think so. Back then mariners could figure latitude accurately, but it took the invention of the chronometer in the mid-1700s to determine longitude. The numbers appeared to be compass bearings. They could be used to triangulate a position, much like cell towers can locate a person." That concept seemed to resonate with Ryan.

"Let's assume they are compass headings," I said. I went into the garage where ancient possessions go to die and found an old paper chart of the north Keys as well as a pair of parallel rulers.

I laid both on the dining table and Ryan said in jest, "Hey, we weren't supposed to take anything else from the Historical Museum!"

"Watch and learn, my young Padawan," I said.

I had to make another assumption. What landmarks did Caesar sight off? There were very few tall trees, and he knew they could be toppled by a hurricane. If I were him, I'd use the island itself. The north and south ends. It was possible they too could be shaped by Mother Nature, but they'd made it this far.

So, I placed the parallel ruler on the chart's compass rose at a heading of 285 degrees. I then walked the ruler to the northern end of the island and drew a long pencil line indicating the sighting. Next, I repeated the process using 197 degrees to the south end. My hands were literally shaking now and I asked Ryan to draw the second line so it intersected the first. And there it was. Several miles off Elliott Key in thirty-five feet of water. I took my old safety compass with attached pencil and drew a half-mile circle around the mark to account for any errors.

Ryan, in turn, was already plotting the lat-lon of our mark into charting software so we could head right to the spot.

~~~

I don't think any of us slept a wink that night. Noelle desperately wanted to join the expedition but had to attend a marine biodiversity conference. I was secretly glad as I wanted her at a distance from our quest. Ryan and I hit the water early the next morning and soon were in the target area. In fact, literally where X marks the spot.

"See anything, Bill?" Ryan was referring to the depth sounder, which showed all manner of bottom features. It even color-coded the objects based on density, so you could tell hard items from soft.

"Nope, not a thing. But remember, if it was easily spotted, it would have been found by now."

We had all our scuba gear on board, but Ryan grabbed his mask and free diving fins and hopped over the side to look around. He would dive to the bottom, scout around, and return to the surface. This went on all day long in an ever-widening circle. I even blew two tanks scouting as my breath wasn't as good as his.

We spent all day searching sand, turtle grass, small patch reefs but found nothing resembling treasure or even a clue. As the sun was setting, we headed in. We even avoided Captain Caesar's
~~~

namesake channel but returned home through the less interesting and unmarked Boca Chita channel.

ELEVEN

Over fried lionfish that night, we reviewed the day's events together. After clearing the dishes, we spread out all our treasure-related materials: the scrimshaw, charts, rulers, etc. We checked and double-checked everything and always came back with the same coordinates.

Around midnight, we were both frustrated and Ryan accidentally poked himself on my old compass. "Ouch," he said. "Why do you keep this old stuff around? It's just varying degrees of old junk."

"Hey, old junk works," I replied tersely. "The Egyptians designed and built a few things out of old junk. Let's see you and your tablet figure that out. Varying degrees of old, my ass." I wasn't mad, but I was tired, so I headed off to bed. "Not too late, Ryan, okay?"

"Okay," came the reply.

"Old varying degrees," I muttered as I walked down the hallway. "Varying old degrees. Variance in degrees of old! That's it. Ryan, that's it! You did it!" I screamed.

Ryan bluntly replied, "Do you know Molly?"

"Huh? No. But listen to the old guy, okay? Compasses point to the magnetic North Pole, not the geographic North Pole."

"Yes, I know," said Ryan. "We covered that in kindergarten."

I let that go but continued. "Yes, but did they tell you that the magnetic North Pole moves around?"

"No."

"Well, it does and it certainly wasn't in the same place three hundred years ago as it is today. So, Caesar's bearings were based on where the magnetic pole was in his day, not today, three hundred years later."

"Holy shit," Ryan said. I let that go too as we were hot on the trail once again!

I continued. "It's called variation, and navigational users must adjust their calculations for it. For instance, let's say you wanted to travel a course due east but the variation is one degree. This means you must steer ninety-one degrees by the compass to adjust for the difference. But in today's world we rely on GPS to compute our location and headings, not compasses. But when you said, 'varying degrees of old,' I remembered the term from reading my *Chapman Piloting & Seamanship* book. Fire up your computer and start researching. I'm goin' to bed. I can't keep your crazy hours," I joked.

I lay awake in bed with my mind in overdrive. The possibility of our quest reaching fruition would impede sleep for anyone. As my mind pondered all the details of the upcoming search, another question maneuvered itself to the forefront.

Why had Ryan hijacked the Coast Guard drone? I believe he had had altruistic motives, but there was also something unsaid. He was a complicated boy and when the time was right, I would pursue this further.

I woke at 6 a.m., tired and excited. Ryan was at the kitchen table, sipping black coffee and glowing with pride. "I did it," he said proudly. "I found a doctoral research paper online that outlines the variation for 1700 to 1720 in the North Atlantic area. I then adjusted the headings, used your crazy parallel rulers, and voilà. A new search area."

TWELVE

I stared at the chart and, sure enough, the new target area was several miles away from our prior one. I knew it was no use postponing our trip, as Ryan and I were beyond excited. So, we packed the boat and once again headed east through Caesar's Creek for our second treasure hunt. Ryan was sound asleep on our dive bags within minutes.

We started at the center of the new search area and damn if it wasn't right on top of George's reef. *This can't be.* Ryan and I silently put on our scuba gear and dove overboard. We scoured the area just like we'd done when he'd first found the coins. We weaved our way through clouds of colorful fish, gardens of lavender and pink soft corals and the aptly named fire coral waiting to inflict a burn on unprotected skin. We poked our noses into every nook and cranny in the reef. Nothing. Except for a pissed-off moray eel whose nap we interrupted.

After we burned half a tank each, I motioned for Ryan to sit with me on the flat-topped rock for a minute. To the ever-curious mutton and hog snappers, we must have resembled Rodin's *Thinker*. In duplicate. We sat there, lost in thought, accompanied by reef sounds and our silvery compressed air bubbles.

I had a hunch. I motioned for Ryan to hand me

his dive knife. I insisted he carry it, not for protection from denizens, but to free him from being tangled in fishing line. He handed me the knife and I scraped the algae off the rock we were sitting on. There it was. A crude turtle carved into the top. I saw Ryan's saucer eyes through his mask, and we surfaced.

"Holy shit, could it be?"

"Let's find out."

We went back on board the boat and I made a bridle out of spare anchor chain. Ryan swam down and wrapped it around the rock. Then he tied a line to it that was also attached to the boat's stern cleat. His last task was to grab the primary anchor and bring it up. Once on board I fired up our twin 250s and began to slowly pull the rock. After pulling for a few seconds I sent Ryan back over.

He came back speechless. His mouth opened and closed. But no sound came out. Like a silent movie. He comically resembled a goliath grouper sitting by a wreck. I hopped in and he was speechless for a reason. The rock had been covering a hole. A hole with small wooden casks. Some were broken. And there were gold doubloons everywhere. Just like Ryan had found the other day.

"We did it! We found Caesar's treasure!" And I started bawling underwater. Maybe a first in scuba history. "We found it, George! We fuckin'-A found it!!"

We surfaced together and hugged. I don't

know who was happier, me or Ryan. But then my practical side took over.

I said, "Ryan we're breaking about five dozen laws and frankly, I don't care. But first things first. We need a larger boat and a plan." So, we wrestled one barrel aboard and then pulled the rock back in place.

Back at the house we discussed our next steps. My first thought was to recover the gold at night. It was lobster season, so boats operating at night weren't unusual. And the darkness would hide our real mission. The next problem was the boat. I needed something big enough to carry the heavy gold and owners that I could trust with my life. And Ryan's.

Favor time. R & W Florida Seafood had the perfect vessel. A thirty-five-foot lobster boat, named the *Miss Shugana*, that was a beast and even had a powerful hoist. Rob and Walt, the owners, and I shared a few adventures back in the proverbial day.

The most notable was when Walt had gotten us a berth on board the *Wanderlust*, a 120-foot schooner that was searching for shipwrecks and treasure in the Turks and Caicos Islands. The pay was awful, but the chow and chance for adventure were good. We were having a great time until one night all hell broke loose. There are two things you never want to hear in the middle of the night. The first is, "The condom broke." The second is, "Abandon ship, abandon ship!"

We met anxiously on deck near the stern and the Wanderlust was going down fast. Luckily, she had several life rafts and everyone got off safely. There was no time for a mayday call, and in those days, there were no GPS locators, EPIRBs or sat phones. We drifted for two and a half days, baking in the sun with no food or water, until we landed on a small island whose inhabitants rescued us. It took a while but we eventually figured out what happened that night. The captain had opened the seacocks and intentionally scuttled her for the insurance money. He figured we would all be fine in the life rafts. Walter ran into him one night in Marsh Harbor. The captain talks with a pronounced lisp now.

Nothing bonds people more than spending a few nights together on the open ocean, so I gave Rob and Walt a call. An hour later they were sitting in my living room. After some catching up, I said, "Well, Ryan and I found something interesting off Elliott Key this morning. Hey, Ryan, bring it in." Ryan wheeled in a hand truck with the still-dripping cask on it. He took the top off with just the right amount of fanfare.

You should have seen their faces. So, I explained everything over Key lime pie and more than a few greenies. Eventually we came up with a plan. And they were all in.

THIRTEEN

In three days, we were set. There would be a full moon that would help with the underwater visibility.

Ryan and I met my buddies at their processing house on the Miami River. As we gathered our gear I couldn't help but contemplate the history of this now largely commercial river. Just two hundred years ago, Native Americans were plying its waters in dugout cypress canoes to trade at the eastern mouth. Its name meant Sweet Water in the language of one of the many Native American tribes that had called the area home. Sadly, if you took a sip now, the first thing out of your mouth would not be "yum … sweet water."

The trip south would take about an hour or two, which gave me time, too much time, to reflect on our grand adventure. We were on a mission and I wasn't in the mood to clutter my mind with complicated feelings, so I distracted myself by observing the waterborne sights along the way. We passed southward under the William Powell Bridge and the remnants of its drawbridge predecessor, which is now used by fishermen and nighttime shrimpers on an outgoing tide.

To the east, the setting sun reflected off the Golden Dome of the Miami Seaquarium. This old-school Miami attraction brought back memories of the *Flipper* television show, which was partially filmed there. I could hear the theme song now.

> *They call him Flipper, Flipper, faster than lightning, No one you see, is smarter than he, And we know Flipper, lives in a world full of wonder, Flying there under, under the sea! Everyone loves the king of the sea*

Bud, Sandy, Porter Ricks, their father and park ranger, and of course Flipper, all appeared in our living room Saturday nights at 7:30 on NBC. Each episode filled my head with corny saltwater adventures. In hindsight, they probably provided a much-needed counterbalance to the truly crazy adventures I undertook with George.

Soon we passed the location of Richard Nixon's summer White House on Key Biscayne and then turned eastward through Stiltsville, another iconic Miami site. Stiltsville is a collection of wooden houses built on … yes, stilts, in shallow water on both sides of a deepwater channel leading into south Biscayne Bay. Sadly, with each passing hurricane their numbers dwindle.

We then headed south again on our final leg of this crazy journey. As if to accentuate our excitement, we were joined by several playful and smiling dolphins who seemed to enjoy *Miss Shugana*'s bow wave immensely.

We hit the reef at sunset and Ryan and I

descended into the warm water. Everything appeared normal, except there was some kind of movement on the bottom. A dark, moving line. Confused, we kicked to the bottom and saw it was a parade of lobsters walking away from the reef. Sort of like an underwater elephant walk, but instead of trunk to tail, this crustacean conga line used their antennae to keep tabs on the fan tail of its preceding associate.

Why are they leaving? I wondered. *Could it be these fellows and their ancestors have been guarding the treasure for three hundred years? And with its pending recovery they're moving on?* I know it sounds crazy, but given all that had happened, I couldn't discount this theory. Now I felt guilty for grabbing so many of these treasure-guarding sentinels. Or perhaps I need to cut back on the Cuban coffee and get more sleep.

Ryan poked me and we began the recovery operation. The turtle rock was dragged aside and we started to work. Using slings attached to the beefy hydraulic winch, we moved the casks topside without a hitch. As the last barrel went up, I looked over the hole with my dive light. It was hard to see, but there in a corner was a small wooden tablet, covered in wax, which I shoved in my BC. The whole operation took less than three hours, including a short decompression stop for me and Ryan.

~~~
~~~

On the way in, we were all grinning like fools. Of course, we took Caesar's Creek home, and when we were abreast of the pirates' likely campsite, I asked Walt to cut the engine and drift with the incoming tide. With the diesel off, you could hear the gurgling current sweep us along. It was a beautiful night. Almost indescribable. The moon, now in the west sky, was so bright you could read a book or perhaps a treasure map by it. The sea air, absent the day's humidity, was sweet and salty. Like saltwater taffy. No, like dark chocolate with sea salt.

In the mangroves I could make out the silhouettes of grey herons and the moon reflected off the eyes of raccoons eyes in the trees and alligators in the water. We were now abreast of where the camp might have been. I pictured the pirates sitting around a campfire, retelling the day's adventures, sipping grog. I imagined Caesar and wondered if a Native American had joined them. How would they communicate?

I sat on the bow for a moment, shut down my brain and opened my heart. Inwardly I said, *Thank you, Caesar. Whoever you were, wherever you are. Thanks, not just for the treasure, but for bringing me back to life. George was a great mentor and Ryan certainly relit my fire. But without you and your deeds, I wouldn't be here. You paid a great price for your adventures, and if there was a Native American with you—well, I suspect he and his people paid a price too."*

Then an idea started to germinate. It quickly blossomed into a full-bloomed plan. The others might not like it, but I knew in my heart and soul it was the right thing. The only thing.

Then a blast of cold air hit us, seemingly to confirm my thoughts. The same kind of blast that precedes a thunderstorm when downdrafts send the freezing air at fifty thousand feet downward, pancaking into the earth, then fanning out in all directions. We all looked at each other, wondering where it came from. There certainly were no storms about and the night sky was clear.

Eerie. Not to mention I felt like we had eyes upon us. Not ancient eyes, but modern.

We eventually made it back to the house with all the barrels and literally didn't know what to do next. Ryan was washing the dive gear and found the wooden tablet. It too had symbols carved into it, but time and salt water had seeped in and damaged the wood. He later suggested that perhaps Professor DeSolle and her team could restore and decipher the message.

Walt and Rob were growing anxious, understandably, so I thanked them profusely and gave them each ten doubloons. Their transformation back to lobstermen from treasure hunters was a bit reluctant, but necessary.

Later that night, after dinner, I said, "Ryan, when we were drifting through Caesar's Creek earlier, I was hit with a momentous thought. That treasure isn't ours. It was probably stolen from

Native Americans who were enslaved and killed for it." I let that sad picture hang a minute, then continued. "Why don't we give it back to them? And not to rich casino Native Americans, but indigenous people. Primitive people who need to be protected from the so-called civilized world."

"Well, that's just weird," Ryan replied.

I was taken aback by his comment and more than a little hurt. I'd thought he had more compassion. I countered sternly with, "Why is that weird?"

"Cuz I was thinking the exact same thing." So, we stayed up most of the night, making phone calls and writing emails. Another cockamamie plan was hatched.

FOURTEEN

The next morning, Phil the Landscaper rolled up at dawn, as he did every day during mango season. To an observer it looked like Ryan and Phil were going through their usual routine of transporting five-gallon buckets of mango gold to the fruit stand. Except today, the buckets were filled with the real deal.

Once the heavily laden buckets were loaded, we headed past the stand, then north to Opa Locka airport. Made sense that our fanciful journey continued onward in a city based on the theme of Ali Baba and flying carpets. It was a different world now and there was real airport security. Phil handed the guard an authorization letter for his newly retained landscape service, courtesy of Ryan's skills. The guard poked around the truck and trailer a bit, but we'd covered the buckets with a layer of mulch to deter prying eyes.

I directed Phil around a couple of old blimp hangars until we arrived at our destination. There she was! The ol' Yellowbird. Sure, her bright yellow paint job was now a faded sepia, which seemed appropriate as by aeronautical standards she was quite ancient. Her engines, though, were still oddly shiny and black. "Can you believe it?" I exclaimed to Ryan. "We got the ol' Yellowbird!

What a beaut!"

Ryan was astonished, but I don't think in a good way. I said, "Look, a chartered Gulfstream was outside our budget and frankly they required a degree of paperwork and scrutiny we couldn't pass."

We both turned to the waving pilot, who was descending the boarding ladder to meet us. Then he drunkenly stumbled to the ground right in front of us. Uh-oh. The apple doesn't fall far from the tree. Or should I say lime. Ryan knew the story of our drunken flight and was now very skeptical. Thank goodness he popped up soberly and said, "Damn, I need to fix that step. Bill? Hi, I'm Captain Bob. You flew with my father, Captain Rick."

"Glad to meet you, and thanks for flying in on short notice."

"No problem. My dad said I'd hear from you one day. And any friend of George is a friend of Yellow Bird Air."

"Say hello to my son Ryan. He's an explorer in training."

"Great to meet you, kid. Hey, got any mangoes? I'm plumb out." As if he'd expected the question, Ryan promptly produced a couple from his cargo pockets. "Great! Nothing beats a sweet mango at ten thousand feet."

"Listen," I said, "we're kind of in a hurry here."

"Yeah, yeah."

So, Bob opened the side cargo door, and we

commenced the transfer. As we did so, I heard sirens in the distance. They couldn't be for us, but in an abundance of caution I suggested we hurry up. The last of the buckets were loaded and now the sirens were much closer. I could even see the blue lights through the airport's chain-link perimeter fence.

Bob ran up the ladder and started his preflight checklist, which meant thumping the gas gauge with his finger. He turned the ignition on, and the port prop began to slowly rotate but soon stopped. This was followed by a huge bang and a mushroom cloud of black exhaust. He tried it again with the same result. The sirens were closer now.

Bob leaned out the cockpit window and yelled, "Hey, can you lend a brother a hand?" Shit fuck. I ran to the big greasy propeller and yanked as hard as I could. Pop pop then nothing. "Again," Bob yelled. "Pull like your lives depend on it." I redoubled my efforts and nothing. Ryan walked over, apparently to help. What could my skinny techno geek son do?

Except, a summer of diving, fishing, mowing and hauling mangoes had put muscle on him. He had turned into a man overnight. He grabbed the prop, received a thumbs-up from Bob and pulled down with all his might. Pop pop. Rumble rumble. Whhr whrr. The antique Pratt and Whitney radial came unenthusiastically to life in a sputtering cloud of smoke, followed by a rainbow-colored oily mist. The exhaust sounded like Krakatoa, but the engine was running. Ryan sprinted to the starboard engine and repeated the process. Bob yelled over the incredibly loud engine roar, "*Vayan con Dios, amigos!* See ya on the other side." He released the plane's brakes and headed speedily to runway three-niner for takeoff. Okay, I have no idea what runway he was using, but I just wanted to say three-niner.

We were surrounded by several police cars now. The occupants were hugely agitated, as if someone were yanking their collective chain. The leash holder soon appeared. He was short in stature but long in attitude. He approached me and said, "I'm the district attorney for Miami-Dade County. Don't worry, we have a team in Grand Cayman waiting on that flying pile of junk."

So together we watched the Yellow Bird lurch down the runway, leave the ground with the grace of a pregnant albatross and head south over the Straits of Florida.

While this was going on, hard-of-hearing Phil was adding brake fluid to his own relic when one of the officers ordered him to step away. But his back was turned, he didn't hear a thing and the situation escalated quickly. The officer made two demands, unbuckled his Taser, and assumed a firing position.

Ryan stepped between the two and yelled, "He can't hear you," trying to defuse the situation.

But it deteriorated until the high-strung DA yelled, "Tase the fucker!"

The Taser discharged, missed Phil, and hit Ryan square in the chest. He went down and started flopping like a boated fish. The scene would have been comical, but I was scared to death. I rushed to him and, mid-twitch, he looked at me and winked. I was so confused until I saw one of the Taser leads hadn't penetrated his shirt. He was acting. So, I was left with no choice.

"Oh my God," I yelled. "You shot my boy. You fucking idiots shot my boy!"

Now Phil joined in. He might be hard of hearing, but he sized up the situation quickly. Being no fan of law enforcement, he too rendered aid to Ryan. And covertly covered him in bloodlike red brake fluid. For his encore, Ryan stood up, still twitching, covered in phony blood, stared into a nearby security camera and said, "I was just trying to help, Dad. I'm sorry. They shot me. Don't forget to feed Jinxie." Then he collapsed. If he could have stopped his heart like some Indian yogi, he would have. Who knew the kid had such mad acting chops? And who the heck was Jinxie?

~~~

Ryan was eventually cleared by Miami-Dade Fire Rescue and we ended up in a small antiseptic room at the downtown police station. We didn't say much as Ryan made the universal sign for "this place is bugged." Ever get a song stuck in your head? Well, my cranium picked a find time to play
~~~

a snippet of a Warren Zevon song over and over. "Send lawyers, guns, and money! The shit has hit the fan." After an obnoxious wait, our nemesis DA eventually walked in. Bantam rooster style.

"Gentlemen," he said, "my name is Peter Little, and we have a problem." Ryan and I each smiled at each other childishly. Good to see we still had a sense of humor. Little Peter continued, "You've broken over one hundred local, state, and federal laws at last count and frankly must pay the piper. So, I'm prepared to offer you a deal. Ten years for you, five with good behavior, and three years in juvie for young Ryan here."

I knew he was trying to shake us. But not me, not today. I felt like I had three hundred years of salty pirate blood flowing through my veins. He was the one who was in trouble.

"Aren't you related to Dick Little?" I inquired.

"You mean Richard! Yes, I am," he said proudly. "He was my grandfather."

I decided to fire the first broadside. Cannonball. Not grapeshot. Not chain. "You know he was an asshole's asshole. Right?" Kaboom. Direct hit. His face and body language flinched.

He fired back, but off target. "Well, sir, I was prepared to be professional here. Years ago, he told me about you and George Henderson. Real thorn in his side. Interlopers. Trespassers. And now you're corrupting a new generation. My grandfather was a great Miamian. Philanthropic. Guardian of antiquities."

"Let me stop you right there," I interrupted. "He was anti-ecology, anti–Native American, anti–African American. Shit, he was just plain antihuman. What he was… was a money-hungry, cowardly bigot."

"So, you want to fight these charges, do you?"

"Yes, and you'll regret it."

As he exited the small conference room, I said, "I am curious, though—why did you show up at the airport?"

"We were tipped off," he replied. "Perhaps you aren't as smart as you thought. See ya in court."

FIFTEEN

For the next two months we tried to keep our heads down low and our spirits high as we prepared for the upcoming trial. I decided, somewhat idealistically, to represent the two of us without an attorney. Damn the torpedoes, full speed ahead!

Finally, the day of the trial was upon us. It was an incredibly hot and humid day like many in South Florida. The courtroom's air conditioning could not keep up with the flood of people in attendance. Even the normally cool Noelle was looking a little shiny. I sat there with a pile of legal pads in front of me, an ancient laptop and Ryan clicking away on his modern one. Soon the courtroom temp began to improve. Ryan smiled and I didn't ask. AC hacker to the rescue. We were both oddly confident.

The Miami Courthouse was an iconic downtown Miami building constructed in 1925. One if its claims to fame is the presence of hundreds of vultures ever circling its pyramid-shaped rooftop. This obviously led to many lawyer jokes throughout the years. Contradicting its age and lack of physical updates was the remarkable computer infrastructure that the building recently installed throughout the building. In fact, Peter Little prided himself on bringing the state attorney's office into the twenty-first century. High def monitors, blazing high-speed internet, surround sound. Resources that Ryan and I planned to take full advantage of. Like modern-day techno pirates.

That's not true. Drunk tourists on Ocean Drive were "taken advantage of" with fifty-dollar drink specials. We weren't going to just take advantage of Peter Little. We were going to destroy Peter Little. Get him disbarred. He would suffer a lack of marital consortium. We'd hold him upside down and give him a swirly in a bus station restroom. With his own toys. We were Solvers of Ancient Legends. Not mere defendants. Little Peter had no idea who he was messing with, but I guarantee you he'd never forget this defense dream team.

The State's table had three attorneys in addition to Peter Little. They too had tablets clicking away with the intimidating intent of incarcerating me and Ryan. Unknown to them, however, was that Ryan might or might not have made some forays into the state attorney's servers. My real attorney insisted I add that disclaimer.

The state attorney strolled cockily to center stage and started the proceedings.

"Ladies and gentlemen, this father and son team are charged with numerous crimes, including impersonating a licensed air-conditioning mechanic, contributing to the delinquency of a minor, theft of Native American artifacts, including a limestone turtle, lying to a police officer, unauthorized access of various computer networks, theft of rum barrels, theft of historically designated treasure…"

I zoned out until I heard, "Lastly, Your Honor, we believe this duo was aided by a third person on the rooftop of the Miami Museum Building. But we have not located them yet."

I looked at Ryan and he at me. We were almost proud of the litany of crimes we committed. But this was a serious affair and I could not let any mirth intrude into the proceedings. Well, not yet.

While Little was reading the trumped-up charges, the first of Ryan's barrages hit the prosecution team's laptops. They all went blank and then the following appeared.

> *Lawyers, beware!*
> *You're in Black Caesar's waters now.*
> *Leave now or accept your fate!*
> *Keel haul or walk the plank!*
> *You decide, mateys.*
> *I offer no quarter.*
> *Govern yourselves accordingly.*

The three looked at each other, speechless. By the time they processed what had happened, the salty message disappeared and the screens returned to their normal state of Word docs, PDFs, rulings, briefs, PowerPoint files. The usual digital legal arsenal.

Then it was my turn. I said, "Ladies and gentlemen of the jury, these charges are ludicrous, and I believe are a result of a personal vendetta by the state's attorney, Mr. Little Peter." Snickers from the peanut gallery. "Excuse me, Mr. Peter Little. Well, perhaps I did briefly impersonate a licensed AC mechanic." But with a smile I dryly added, "But haven't we all at one time or another?" That produced a slight chuckle from the jury members, at which the judge rapped lightly with his gavel. "I won't waste your time," I continued. "The charges are preposterous. Let's get this trial over with. And perhaps we'll all make happy hour. Mojitos on me!" Again, a slight chuckle. I had them eating out of my hand.

It was now Little's turn to present his case. But he and his associates were tapping furiously at their keyboards. They had enigmatically gone blank. They stared daggers at Ryan, who just kept up his steadfast typing on his laptop. I recalled the words of Lord Nelson, naval hero of the Battle of Trafalgar. No captain can go wrong if he lays his ship alongside his enemy. Well, we couldn't get any closer and Ryan was apparently launching broadside after digital broadside. To further frustrate Little and his team, they weren't allowed to bring up Ryan's past digital transgressions.

Little started to ask the judge for a brief recess to fix their issues when an associate coughed and indicated they were up and running. It was all downhill from there. His high-def monitors would slowly go blank, the picture would turn upside down, fade to gray, turn psychedelic.

Little was slowly becoming unglued. The only person more frustrated than him was the judge, who hated all this high-tech stuff and was unaware of Ryan's, shall we say, prowess.

Before he blew a cranial gasket, Little asked for an early lunch recess, which the judge gladly granted. In the hallway, we met Noelle, who had thoughtfully brought some sandwiches and a few slices of Key lime pie, which we ate quickly in the hallway.

She left us alone for a minute to get some drinks and I said to Ryan, "Hey, I've been thinking about the drone."

"Yes?" he questioned.

"Well, I know you meant well, but it seems a pretty obscure piece of equipment to target and apply your skills towards. And the risk, well, the risk is crazy." I didn't press him any further and we both sat silent.

He next said, "It's the dreams, Bill, my dreams. My nightmares."

"Huh?" I said. "You never have nightmares."

"Yes, I do. I've always had them. I just never told anyone."

"Well, tell me now, we have some time."

"They've been a part of me as long as I can remember. I'm alone in the ocean. It's stormy and dark. The waves are gigantic and there's boat wreckage everywhere. I'm close to drowning. Someone or something is trying to help me. Like they're throwing a rope or extending an oar. But it's always just out of reach. I'm scared for myself. I'm scared I'll never see family or friends again."

"And you don't want others to suffer a reality like that?"

"Well, kind of. Sure, I want to help anyone I can. But I also thought if I fixed the drone properly the nightmares would end." With that, I gave him the best hug a man could give a son.

Noelle walked up and it turned into a communal hug. "It will be all right," she whispered, and we replied in unison, "Yes, it will."

We returned to the almost empty courtroom to find Little's IT guru going over the laptops. He eventually said, "I can't find anything wrong with them, but I brought three more. I can have them up and running in thirty minutes."

Little gruffly said, "You have twenty," and walked angrily over to me and Ryan.

As he approached, Ryan closed his laptop guiltily and Little spat out, "I know you're behind this, boy. I know your past. Orphan hacker. Mango stealer. Juvie aspirant." Ryan remained maturely nonchalant, but I didn't.

I stood and put my arm around Little's shoulder in what looked like a friendly gesture and slowly whispered, "Say one more word about my son—one more fucking word—and this will turn into a different kind of trial."

Ryan kicked me from under the table and Little took a wobbly step back. Ryan now stood up and said to the IT guy, "Hey, Larry, after you download your data, disconnect the Wi-Fi and cellular connection—then you'll know it can't be me. Perhaps a glitch in your back-office servers?"

You couldn't help but notice a touch of admiration in the abused IT guy's face. Ryan knew his name. Ryan might not have street cred, but apparently, he had web cred in spades. Little glared at his IT guy and said, "Well?"

"He has a point."

"Then do it, goddamn it."

When the trial resumed, the judge asked me if that was homemade Key lime pie we'd enjoyed in the hallway. "Of course, Your Honor. Is there any other kind?"

"When we're done here, let's compare recipes," he said judiciously.

Little then resumed his Clarence Darrow impersonation. But this Darrow had taken the brown acid, and Dalí had produced his evidentiary materials. Banners with lawyer jokes were running along the bottom of all the associates' laptops. The usual, you know: "What do you call a busload of lawyers going over a cliff? A start." Their attempts to remain stone faced were futile. Like fighting the Borg. Several times they almost burst out in mass laughter. Imagine teenage girls the millisecond before they start a laughing fit.

After Little's pathetic attack, it was our turn. Which I turned down. I told the jury I was taking the high road and not acknowledging his lies, intimidating tactics and amateurish, glitch-filled presentations.

SIXTEEN

The judge looked at me quizzically and then directed Little to begin his closing arguments.

"Ladies and gentlemen of the jury, we have a heinous crime here. No, we have multiple crimes here." As Little yammered on, the jury was trying to view the latest material to pop up on the courtroom monitors. It was Little's law degree. From the Prestigious and Most Highly Enlightened Law School at the University of North Korea. Signed by Kim Jong Un himself! What an honor! He'd graduated summa cum commie.

The diploma disappeared and Little tried to carry on. But he was fixating on Ryan, who was typing furiously. In Little's addled brain, Ryan was preparing the coup de grâce of hacking. And Little's ego couldn't take one more iota from a retired accountant and his boy genius son.

He slyly continued, "Perhaps the real villain here is young Ryan?" he asked and slowly wandered towards our table. Ryan didn't even look up as Little continued. "In fact, ladies and gentlemen, not only was young Ryan the brains behind the entire operation, but he is also responsible for the sabotaging of the district attorney for Miami-Dade County's presentation today, as well as patently thumbing his nose at the basis of our judicial system!"

And with that he snatched up the laptop and proudly held it up high for all to see. Like a vertically challenged Aztec priest with a sacrifice. Or a child angler holding a world-record mutton snapper. Either way, he had nothing to be proud of. So, I stood up and interjected myself into the now silent courtroom. I snatched the laptop back and held it high for all to see the brightly colored playing cards.

I then said, "Well, I don't know what you call that in the state attorney's office. But in my house, we call that a vicious game of solitaire."

Now it was my turn. I returned to my seldom used laptop and hit the F and U keys simultaneously as Ryan had instructed. All eyes were once again on the monitors. The audio came up first. All heard the DA's shrieking voice, "Tase the fucker. Tase the fucker," over and over emanating from dark screens. That soundbite faded into "You shot my boy. You bleeping idiots shot my boy!" Now the screens came to life and morphed into a badly injured Ryan saying, "I was just trying to help, Dad. I'm sorry. They shot me. Don't forget to feed Jinxie for me." Then he collapsed.

Now perhaps the greatest part of the trial occurred. Little running around the courtroom, desperately trying to jump up and unplug all the monitors. Needless to say, the judge ordered a ten-minute recess, in which both sides were treated sternly. But I think he was starting to enjoy the interlude from real law. I know the jury was.

Now it was my turn.

"Ladies and gentlemen, we are accused of a variety of crimes. The most significant being an alleged treasure haul from the waters off Elliott Key. But you should know the real thief was the government of Spain and its legal pirates. They killed, tortured and bribed throughout Central and South America to obtain billions in gold and silver bullion. All to fuel their bankrupt country, their political dreams and just plain greed. And if there was any gold, it surely belongs to the descendants of the miners, slaves and victims of the brutal regime.

"What are we guilty of? We are guilty of solving a three-hundred-year-old mystery and contributing to the historical knowledge of South Florida. And we are not in possession of any alleged treasure. In fact, I challenge the State to produce evidence of any treasure."

As I pondered my next oratorical gem, the rear courtroom door opened and an elderly Seminole gentleman with long white hair entered in a wheelchair. He was wearing his tribe's traditional multicolored jacket and pushed by a young woman with similar hair but black as the collective heart of the Little line.

We made eye contact. He looked familiar. Damn, it was Charlie Cypress. He was here to help, and a new strategy began to form in my mind. Although I thought the jury was clearly on our side, I couldn't take that chance.

"Your Honor, may I approach the bench?"

I made my request and Little and I were soon in the judge's chambers.

The judge said, "Well, this is certainly unorthodox, but then again, this trial is bordering on the absurd. I'm going to hit the head and when I get back I want a resolution here."

I addressed Little. "I understood you have political aspirations. No candidate can win with an albatross around their neck. And Dick Little was such a bird."

Peter said, "I tend to disagree. What do you think my grandfather did?"

"Let's see," I said. "He evicted elderly African Americans from the west Grove. He intentionally damaged the ecosystem on Elliott Key by cutting the Spite Road. He shot at me and George, and … he used ancient five-hundred-year-old Tequesta and Miccosukee pottery for target practice."

"That's absurd. Even if it were true, you have no way of proving anything."

"Perhaps not. The Grove eviction records were on microfiche but were destroyed when Hurricane Andrew flooded a portion of City Hall. And the Spite Road has largely grown back. And it's my word against a ghost's as to shooting at me and George. But destroying priceless ancient artifacts while wearing a homemade police costume? That's heinous. Nobody is voting for the spawn of that person. Demonstrates a lack of family character and just plain stupidity and arrogance."

Little arrogantly said, "Prove it. There were no witnesses."

"Well, that's where you're wrong. Did you see the Seminole gentleman in the rear of the courtroom? He was an employee of your grandfather. He is a tribal elder of the Seminole tribe and member of their Tribal Council. I will bring him in to testify somehow or the Miami *Trib* will do a story. Either way it's your career.

"Look," I said, "don't let your family vendetta against me cloud your judgment. I'll concede to something. Give me community service, but Ryan goes free. We'll turn over the few remaining artifacts for further study. Take the win, the public good will be served and your good name is intact." I winced at that thought.

While Little contemplated my offer, I had one more card up my sleeve.

"Ever visit your grandfather's grave site?"

"Yes."

"How's the smell?"

"God-awful."

"I can make it stop."

His mouth opened to say something stupid, but his brain took over and Little announced there was a settlement to the just returned judge.

As we exited the chambers, I asked Little,

"How did you really find out about us?"

Clearly exhausted he replied, "An Englishman called us. Mondard, Maynard—something like that. He's no fan of yours or Black Caesar for that matter."

~~~

"Ladies and gentlemen of the jury, I thank you for your service. A settlement has been reached and this trial is now over." Under his breath he muttered, "Thankfully."

As Ryan, Noelle and I walked to the rear of the courtroom, we sought out Charlie and his young companion. "I see you're driving a smaller dozer these days."

Charlie smiled and introduced the three of us to his granddaughter, Andrea. "Help me stand, Andrea. This is Billy Finnegan. He is a good man and keeper of many George stories." She was delightful and bright. Full of life. She and an obviously smitten Ryan engaged in teenage small talk while I continued conversing with Charlie.

Charlie had a million questions about Caesar's legend and the treasure. After filling him on the details of our exploits, I made a request.

"Sure, anything, Billy. I am grateful to be a small part of all this. George would be so proud of you. What can I do?"

"Well, if anybody asks, you saw Little use
~~~

Tequesta pottery for target practice."

"Sure, Billy, whatever you say."

SEVENTEEN

The next day we all paid George a visit. The grounds were freshly mowed, and the pleasant smell of chlorophyll drifted in on the breeze. I closed my eyes and I was mowing the back forty at Shangri-La. Strange how you can move through time in the blink of an eye.

"Hi, George. It's me, Billy. You remember Noelle?"

"Hi, George."

"And Ryan?"

"Hi, George."

I started to tear up, but Noelle gripped my hand, and I started, "Well, George, we did it. We found Caesar's treasure. Remember the first reef we ever dove on? It was right under our noses the whole time. Like we were being guided there. Under the flat rock by the two big brain corals. And the limestone turtle was the key. It had a cavity containing instructions to find the treasure. Fifty million dollars' worth. Now here's the crazy part. We gave it all away.

"We broke so many laws, we knew the government would never let us keep it. And after all, it wasn't ours. It belonged to the people who really found it.

"Captain Rick's surprisingly sober son flew the treasure to Cayman Brac in the ol' Yellow Bird.

From there, one of Soto's dive boats snuck it in through North Sound on Grand Cayman to Rum Point. They blended in with all the boats at Sting Ray City. Can you believe that's a tourist attraction now? George, people actually pay money to swim with stingrays! Crazy, huh?

"The treasure was then trucked to George Town. I don't think you'd like what the town turned into, but it served us well. Hundreds of banks. Tens of thousands of offshore corporations. An incredible complex web of international laws and treaties that we were willing to hide behind and they were more than willing to convert the treasure into cash, bearer bonds and even cryptocurrency."

Noelle and Ryan looked at me and both mouthed, "He doesn't know what crypto currency is."

I shrugged and mouthed back, "Shit, neither do I," and continued.

"Then, George, the money was donated to charities assisting indigenous people in Central and South America. They desperately need protection from the civilized world. From people like Richard Little. They and their ancestors suffered horribly. The treasure belongs to them and will go a long way to help protect and preserve their way of life.

"The crazy thing is I don't think Caesar would mind. He had to have coexisted on the island with at least one Tequesta. Heck, he was probably part of the treasure secret. He most likely carved the turtle. Caesar would have trusted him immensely.

So that's that. Thank you, Geor …" I started to tear up again and Noelle gripped my hand a bit harder. "Thank you, George," I continued. "And thank you, Noelle and Ryan. You both have made my life meaningful. This was a great, great journey. More than a man deserves."

I gathered myself and then continued. "But George, we still have a few mysteries to solve. Someone tipped Little's grandson off about us. What's that about? And someone or something put a blue turtle on your headstone. Who or what else is involved?"

With that, Ryan coughed and was looking guilty as hell. I stared at him, and he said sheepishly, "Uh, I put the turtle there. When we left to get flowers. So, it looked like it was placed there while we were gone. It was the same turtle you let me study. I needed to get you motivated and it worked. Please don't be mad."

I wasn't mad. In fact, the opposite was true. Without that motivation I might have let the legend flounder. Once again Ryan had proved he was wise beyond his years.

I continued. "So, George, I hope you're okay with all that? I know it's ridiculous to ask for any kind of sign you approve. It would mean a lot to us, though." Just then a shadow passed overhead and an anhinga landed silently on his tombstone. A water bird oddly far from home. He stared at each of us for a few seconds with dark, quizzical eyes. I've always liked anhingas. Many people regard the flamingo as the iconic South Florida bird. Perhaps due their presence on South Beach, where they could blend in with all the other showy, dim-witted people. But to me the hardworking, smiling anhinga was the true avian ambassador of South Florida. After seemingly staring into our souls, he then took off, leaving a reminder of his appearance on George's headstone.

"That'll work, George."

EIGHTEEN

Turns out the wooden tablet was holding on to its secrets like an Ambrosia hit single. The scrimshaw carvings had slowly disintegrated over time. Lignum vitae may be the toughest wood in the world, but three hundred years underwater was a lot to ask of cellulose. Nevertheless, Noelle and the archaeology department's team from the university kept at it, trying to reconstruct the images using the same techniques as those used to analyze the Shroud of Turin and the Dead Sea Scrolls.

One night I was dropping off fresh stone crabs as a special treat for Noelle and her team when one of her grad students yelled out, "Professor, I think we got it! I've run it through the cryptology algorithm three times. I'm certain it's right. Except for one word, which we can't figure out."

Noelle grabbed the printout and we read it together.

> *Smith, my boy, I knew you'd figure me clues. This here loot was taken from those who had, for those who need, by God. You must use the treasure to get Kalos and his Tekesta people to the Cuban coast. The fishing is good there and they don't need much. 'Tain't right they been kilt and*

moved from their land. Kalos taught me we don't need much to have a good life. Perhaps a wee bit of demon rum. Har har. What's leftover be yours.

Now, laddie, here's some advice from ol' Caesar. Always keep two doubloons with you to remind you that treasure is always near. Your da, may he rest in peace, taught you to be a good blacksmith and I think I learnt you a few things. Some good, some bad. Har har.

Kalos says we will see each other again in Ikanay. I hope so, mate.

I loved you like my own.

Now matey go make ol' Caesar proud and fulfill your dreams!

We all stared at each other in a stupor. Caesar had just leapt from his grave and spoken to us. Being at the junction where science collides with the past is a powerful thing. In Europe there's a seventeen-mile particle accelerator that smashes atoms to pieces, revealing previously undiscovered building blocks of our very existence. This was the enormity of our feeling. The past and the present had just collided to reveal a new emotion within us. The recovery of the treasure was awesome, but I'd felt no real attachment to that past. This was different. We were conversing with a person. A legend. Flesh and blood. Human evolution and our own DNA didn't prepare us for this kind of event.

Ryan spoke first. "Whoa, that's crazy!" he exclaimed. Noelle and I nodded mutely in agreement.

Then his face took on an expression I had never seen. Contemplative and stern. Like he was trying to see inside himself.

"Ryan, are you okay?" I asked.

He replied slowly, "I'm having déjà vu. For real. I'm……I'm on a beach. At night, a long time ago. And I know the word Ikanay. It's a Tequesta word. I should know what it means. It's important. I need my laptop." With that he hurriedly left the room.

Noelle and I didn't get a chance to say anything to Ryan and now we were just standing there in an imposed silence.

My mind was flooding with questions and the hypotheses I'd hated so much in science class. So, there was boy. And a Tequesta. Questions answered and new questions arise. The boy was an orphan blacksmith. And where or what was Ikanay? Why was Ryan so agitated?

Ikanay must be a Tequesta word. But their language had died with that ancient people. An extinct language and an extinct race. How foolish and sad. Imagine the knowledge they'd possessed living here in South Florida for hundreds or even thousands of years. Ryan would search high and low, but he would never find the meaning of Ikanay.

My inquisitive nature moved on. Why would

Caesar leave a message to a boy? There was no place for a boy in this legend. Why was he so important? What could a boy do? I thought. I hesitated. With George's guidance and inspiration, I'd been able to accomplish a lot. And where would we be without Ryan's determination and brains? Nevertheless, pirates wouldn't have boys with them. Would they?

As I pondered all these questions, Herb Albert's relaxing trumpet floated in over the music system. "Memories of Madrid." One of my favorites. Then memories of the Grove entered my mind. Now I was swept suddenly back in time to my mom's avocado-colored living room. She was reading the letter from her friend in the DAR.

"… there was a pirate trial in Williamsburg in 1718 and there's a list of prisoners and their sentences. What colorful names. Paddy Nine Fingers. Spanish Johnny."

"Ma, I don't care about them! Was there a Caesar?"

"I swear you are so impatient, young man."

"I'm sorry, Ma, it's just very important!"

"Let's see. Yes, here it is. It says Captain Caesar, escaped slave. Death by hanging. How horrible. All were convicted and hanged. Except a boy."

My impatient teenage self had heard nothing after she'd mentioned "Captain Caesar…escaped slave." But I could hear her ensuing words now: "Except a boy." So, there was a boy with the pirates. Why wasn't he hanged? I closed my eyes for a second and thought what I would do in Caesar's place. I would do anything for Ryan, that's for sure. Caesar had most certainly made an impassioned appeal for the boy's life.

Noelle looked at me and said, "Are you okay? You have the same look that Ryan had. Like you're trying to see inside yourself."

"I'm okay," I said, but I wasn't. Something was happening inside me, like I was inwardly flying through time.

Noelle eventually said, "I'm concerned about Ryan. Tell me about his folks."

Tearing myself loose from my "time travel," I said, "Well, I know very little about them. They were reenactors, the people who traveled with Renaissance festivals and such. They liked to live in the past. Not cut out for this world."

"How did they die?"

"Propane tank explosion, that's all I know."

My mind began to race. From the Grove to the present. Then back to 1718. There was more to this. I could feel it in my bones. Something or someone was telling me we weren't quite done with the legend.

"Noelle," I said, "can you Google news articles about Ryan's parents' death? It happened near St. Augustine approximately fifteen years ago."

"Sure," she said. A few minutes later she found an article.

"Sue and Harry Cooper. You were right. They died in a propane accident."

"What did they do? Does it say?"

"Yes," she replied. "She was a seamstress and he was a blacksmith."

I thought for a minute and said, "Noelle, do you have access to that drop box thingy in the cloud? Where Ryan scanned all my mom's materials?"

"Sure, why?"

"I'd like to see the list of the pirate defendants."

A few minutes later, the printer hummed and we were staring at it.

Name	Occupation	Sentence
Black Caesar	Captain	Death by hanging
Alexandros "Ulysses" Papadopoulos	First mate	Death by hanging
Alex "Stumps" McKenzie	Boatswain	Death by hanging
Peter "Sad Eyes" Torrance	Helmsman	Death by hanging
Frances "Puddles" McKenzie	Helmsman	Death by hanging
Paddy "Nine Fingers" Barbant	Seaman	Death by hanging
Thomas "Four toes" Willaby	Seaman	Death by hanging

Name	Occupation	Sentence
Henry "Jewels" Thompson	Seaman	Death by hanging
"Spanish" Johnny Gonzalez	Cook	Death by hanging
Ryan "Smith" Cooper	Blacksmith	Prison – One year

Seeing the boy's full name gave me a shudder. Ryan Cooper, nicknamed Smith for being a blacksmith. Wow.

My son. My adopted son. Who'd practically solved the legend by himself and had the same name as its intended recipient. Both of their fathers were blacksmiths and both had left their sons' lives prematurely. C'mon, what are the effing chances?

I looked back on the slew of improbabilities that had to occur or the legend would have never been solved.

What were the chances of ...
George meeting the Neidhauks?
Finding the ring?
Surviving a tropical storm in a twenty-one-foot boat?
Finding Noelle again?
Deciphering the mirror imaged Tuareg symbols and finding the treasure?

Were there forces at work here that we would never understand? Nor were meant to? There truly was a mysterious guiding hand constantly pushing us to find the treasure. And to return it to its rightful heirs.

And what of the word Ikanay? This was not the first time I'd heard it spoken. I didn't tell Noelle or Ryan, but I too felt a stirring in my soul upon hearing it said aloud.

Noelle and I next discussed if we should tell Ryan about our findings. We both agreed to wait. Although his maturity and intellect were off the chart, he was still only fifteen. All these secrets, legends and ghosts had waited this long. Ryan's wait would be a bit longer.

EPILOGUE: PART ONE

Summer 1718
Post-hurricane
Elliott Key, Florida

Kalos returned gradually to his devastated island world. He'd expected a wind and water hell, but not the hurricane nightmare that enveloped his island home. Lashing himself to the limestone turtle had saved his life. It was the most solid object on the island. A tree limb hit his head at the peak of the storm, and he had been semiconscious ever since. It was not altogether a terrible state, as his body was dulled to the pain of flying debris, and more importantly it allowed his mind to wander unencumbered. In this condition he felt a fading presence on the island, but it remained partially hidden among the death and destruction. He slowly untied the leather lashings and yearned for some of Caesar's strong coffee to clear his head.

He surveyed the remnants of his camp, which was stripped bare and covered in seaweed and dying sea life. He had heard stories of such a storm but not in his lifetime. He worried about his family inland. The animals would have warned them, but of course nothing is certain.

There it was again. That feeling. He stood up and ran to the beach. It was almost impassable with debris. He came across an injured loggerhead turtle on her back and half buried in sand. He flipped the giant over, said a prayer and showed her a path to the ocean, where she could recuperate from her wounds. He then resumed, working his way southward, amazed at the horrible metamorphosis the island had undergone. But here on the beach, he observed one of the peculiar attributes of a hurricane passed.

The sea air was different now. Clean, pure. A hint of ozone, but like nothing he could recall. He breathed deeply, filling his lungs with life. The clouds were different too. The shapes were familiar, but now they were etched in silver against the bluest sky he had ever seen. Vivid and few. The world he knew was gone and replaced with a new one. He was content, though. A cycle had been completed. An unending succession of birth, life, death and rebirth. Nature's Möbius strip. He felt alive and full of renewal and hope. He had a purpose. He had a path that was uncompromising and eternal.

His contemplation was broken by the sound of moaning coming from under a mat of yellow-brown Sargasso seaweed. He dug furiously until he uncovered a seemingly lifeless body. It was Smith and he was entangled in the lines of the shattered dinghy. He too had lashed himself to a lifesaving object. Smart boy. But his body had endured many injuries including a horrible broken leg where the bone had pierced the skin.

Kalos whispered softly, "You made it back, young Smith. You did what Caesar asked. You did well." Smith started to mumble that Caesar had saved him, but Kalos stopped him and said, "Eat this," and he gently placed a gooey paste of ground coontie root in his mouth.

While Smith slowly chewed, Kalos found several tree limbs, which he tied together and then placed Smith on the makeshift travois. With this arrangement he was able to drag the boy back to what was left of his camp. Thankfully, he kept his fire-starting materials in a small, oiled leather bag and they were not waterlogged. He started a small fire next to Smith and gave him water and more root paste. Kalos began to tend to Smith's many injuries. But he feared he could not save him from the inevitable.

Later that day, Smith revived enough to have a short conversation. He told Kalos about the voyage northward, the battle and the demise of Blackbeard and Caesar. Kalos did not seem surprised by any of the tale, but it did have a draining effect on him.

Near the end of the story, Smith revealed Caesar last instructions. "Kalos, Caesar told me to return here and find you. That you would give me the wood scrimshaw. He carved instructions to find the treasure. To safeguard his message, he said only someone clever would be able to interpret them. Without the scrimshaw, the treasure would be lost forever. Do you have it? I promised him,

Kalos. I promised."

Kalos stared into the boy's heart. So strong. Such will he possessed. No wonder Caesar had loved him. He would have made a fine Tequesta. "Here, young Smith. Here's the scrimshaw. You hold it." Kalos laid the carved wooden rod on Smith's chest, which he held on to tightly. Smith felt the symbols in his hands but was too tired to lift his head to see them.

"You should have seen him, Kalos. He commanded respect at that charade of a trial. And when he stood on the gallows, he seemed to savor the moment of his last command. And he saved me, Kalos. They would have been happy to hang a pirate boy. But he saved me. All my shipmates did. Why did they die, and I lived?"

Smith lapsed again into unconsciousness. Kalos felt his head and he knew his blood was on fire. In Kalos's religion one of Smith's three souls was starting to wander, but in Western medicine, an infection had taken hold in his broken leg. And nothing could stop it.

Kalos knew he could not save the boy, but when he was awake, they spent the time talking under the night sky.

"Do you know how Caesar was taken from Africa?"

"Yes, I do."

"Please tell me," Smith asked weakly.

Kalos went on. "Ser'ada, as he was known, and his people were an inland people. They rarely visited the coast. But the coastal villages are where commerce and trade occurred. He traveled to a city called Sherbro with his teenage sons Aksil and Aderfi. They needed supplies including the indigo dye used to color their clothing."

Smith said, "Sons? He never mentioned sons."

Kalos replied, "It was too painful for him to recall their memory. He loved them dearly. When they arrived, the boys went to explore the sights and sounds while Ser'ada traded and bartered. After a few hours he concluded his business and went searching for the boys. As he neared the docks, he found Aksil disheveled and hysterical. Aksil hysterically told his father that slavers had taken his brother Aderfi. He'd fought them, but the slavers had won.

"Ser'ada ran to the dock and stood tall and strong next to the slovenly slave ship. He slowly unwound his tagelmust and roared for the cowardly captain to show himself. When the captain finally appeared, Ser'ada proposed a trade. Himself for the boy. After a brief negotiation, the exchange was accomplished and Ser'ada left Africa. Never to see his sons again.

"On board the hellish ship he became consumed with a need for vengeance. This need kept him alive on the horrifying trip across the ocean, despite the sweltering heat, chains, disease and hunger. It kept him alive, this need for revenge, right up until the time they were shipwrecked. His vengeance was partially satiated while he held the slaver captain's head underwater till he stopped struggling and the last bubble of air escaped his lips.

"We spent many nights discussing revenge and other topics. Before his enslavement, he was a religious man. He knew he had violated one of his God's rules. His religion believed if one was wronged and responded with patience and forgiveness, this behavior was rewarded. Eventually, he made peace with the world, his God and himself, but we will never know.

"When Ser'ada happened upon you, he was reminded of the sons he left behind. He told me so. He was proud of you. He wanted to give you a new life away from pirating."

"Thank you, Kalos. He never told me. I'm cold. Is there any more wood for the fire?"

Kalos threw on some driftwood and then retrieved Ser'ada's tagelmust. "Here, young Smith, put this on." He gently lifted the boy's head and wrapped the now-faded blue cloth around him.

"Look at me, Kalos, I am Tuareg," he said wearily, but with a smile. They sat in silence until Smith said, "Kalos, I fear I won't be able to fulfill the captain's wish. I am too weak. Can you help me? I don't want to let him down."

"Of course I will, young Smith. It would be my honor to help you."

Again, they sat in silence, their faces lit softly by the small driftwood fire. Abruptly Smith's expression became grave, and he said with sudden strength and conviction, "Kalos, I need to stand! Please help me."

Kalos did so, reluctantly, knowing the horrible pain the cracked bone would cause. But he understood why. He helped the boy up, and the sight of Smith grimacing caused Kalos's eyes to tear.

They stared upward, Smith leaning on Kalos, in awe of the innumerable blinking stars set against the blackest of black skies. Few people on earth ever survived an Armageddon to witness such a sight. Another ironic and beautiful aftermath of a large hurricane. For all its destructiveness, it provided an unequaled visual pathway to the heavens. They could each see to the beginning and end of time. Both knew their paths. Clear and pure as this night sky.

"I need to stand by myself, Kalos." And Smith planted both legs steadfast in the ground. Using the scrimshaw rod as a staff, he slowly unwound the deep blue headdress and roared to the heavens, "I am Ryan Cooper, by God! I am Tuareg, son of Ser'ada Ag Ilou. I am not afraid to meet my maker. But by God, I will fulfill my father's wishes. Ser'ada was a great man. A prince he was. A great teacher and a great father. I will love him forever." His words rippled outward as a dropped pebble would in a universal pond. Then the scrimshaw staff fell from his hand, he collapsed and passed on, succumbing to the snake in his blood.

Kalos wept for Cooper. Then he proclaimed to

the still body whose soul was now wandering free, "Yes, you are young Cooper. You are Tuareg. And you are Tequesta. You too will be a great teacher and a great father. You will return and fulfill Ser'ada's wishes. I will see to that. That's my solemn promise to him and my oath to you. We will see each other again, my young friend. Here in Ikanay."

EPILOGUE: PART TWO

So, what happened to our motley crew of legend solvers? I wish I could tell you that it all worked out and I married Noelle and began a life that people only dream about.

So, I fuckin'-A will!

Noelle and I were married under George's gumbo-limbo tree by a shaman who told us there was an abundance of duppies, spirits and very nosy ghosts around. One had a propensity to moon the crowd in attendance. Gee, who could that be? The dinner entrée was Shadow Bree Ond, with Key lime pie for dessert.

Ryan started several software companies. With Andrea Cypress. One in particular assists archaeologists by researching compass variations in ancient maps. The company name ... Pirate Map Software.

Noelle was promoted to head of her department at the university and continues to this day to investigate, shall we say, archaeological oddities.

The missing Coast Guard drone? Well, it reappeared under very mysterious circumstances. Go figure! As the caretaker opened Coral Castle one foggy morning, the drone slowly descended from the sky. An eerie high-tech apparition landing next to the intricately carved limestone observatory. Another fascinating chapter in the attraction's enigmatic history. The drone's operating system had been revamped and the hardware connections received titanium shielding making it impervious to hackers. In contrast to the sudden appearance of the drone was the equally sudden disappearance of Ryan's nightmares.

The Historical Museum? Yeah … we're not allowed in there. They were pretty upset with me and Ryan. Until their admissions skyrocketed. Everyone wanted to see the beautiful Tequesta Turtle. But we're still not allowed inside. Especially if the AC breaks.

I almost forgot about little Peter. This is good shit. He got swept up in the #MeToo movement. With an unfortunate PETA angle. His grandfather, Dick Little, left him a small farm in the Redlands—South Florida's agricultural area. That's right. He was a baaahhhhddd man.

Me? I came out of retirement and founded Two Doubloons Consulting. I'm a professional speaker and motivator, teaching the virtues of being grateful, living a full life and always seeing the treasure around you.

Are you curious about the word Ikanay, the one Noelle's research team couldn't solve?

It's a beautiful word.

One of the first Kalos taught me.

It's a Tequesta word that means "Our Land blessed by the Sun, the Moon and their Children the Stars."

Now matey go and make ol' Caesar proud…
and fulfill your dreams! Har har!

The End … or is it?

I hope you enjoyed reading Pirate's Promise. It was my honor to write it for you!

Visit bwilliamhoolihan.com for interesting tidbits about the people and places mentioned in the book.

If you enjoyed "Pirate's Promise" and want to read more, please e-mail me at bwh@bwilliamhoolihan.com *and let me know your thoughts.*

Oh, and Bill, Noelle, and Ryan would appreciate it, if you give Pirate's Promise a five-star review!!

B. William Hoolihan

ABOUT THE AUTHOR

B. William Hoolihan was born into a world steeped in storytelling. His grandfather, a masterful teller of tales, grew up in rural Kentucky in the early 1900s. Letters describing his childhood adventures on Uncle George's farm first ignited a passion for storytelling in young Bill.

During Bill's formative years, his mother—a single parent and schoolteacher—surrounded him with a vibrant tapestry of adventurous and colorful characters who further inspired him. She nurtured his thirst for adventure by taking him on a journey to the Middle East. Together, they explored the Valley of the Kings, swam in the Dead Sea, and roamed the ancient ruins of the Parthenon. His quest for adventure deepened as he absorbed tales of distant lands and seas, particularly the Caribbean, told by a family friend.

These days, Bill can be found cycling through the back roads of Florida, contemplating new stories and adventures to chronicle. If you see him, feel free to say hello, but tread carefully—you might just become a character in his next tale!